1970

THE ARAB LIST

ALSO AVAILABLE BY **THE AUTHOR**

The Turban and the Hat
Translated by Bruce Fudge

Ice
Translated by Margaret Litvin

RECENT TITLES IN **THE ARAB LIST**

Salim Barakat
The Universe, All at Once
SELECTED POEMS
Translated by Huda J. Fakhreddine

Akram Alkatreb
The Screams of War
SELECTED POEMS
Translated by Jonas Elbousty

Ghassan Zaqtan
An Old Carriage with Curtains
Translated by Samuel Wilder

Hussein Barghouthi
The Blue Light
Translated by Fady Joudah

SONALLAH IBRAHIM

1970
The Last Days

Translated by
ELEANOR ELLIS

LONDON NEW YORK CALCUTTA

The Arab List
SERIES EDITOR: Hosam Aboul-Ela

Seagull Books, 2024

Originally published in Arabic as *1970*
© Sonallah Ibrahim, 2019

First published in English translation by Seagull Books, 2024
English translation © Eleanor Ellis, 2024

ISBN   978 1 8030 9 248 5

British Library Cataloguing-in-Publication Data
A catalogue record for this book is available from the British Library.

Typeset by Seagull Books, Calcutta, India
Printed and bound in the USA by Integrated Books International

1970

1 January

Israeli airstrike on the city of Irbid leaves
11 Jordanians dead, including 6 children.

The US Military Assistance Command in
South Vietnam announces that there were
9,250 US soldiers killed, 69,000 wounded,
and 470 planes and 1,000 helicopters lost
during the last year.

Belly dancer Nahed Sabry was unable to perform on
New Year's Eve as promised due to an injury in her
left metatarsus. She danced in 19 of 23 events she
was hired for. Dr Yahia al-Katib gave her two
stitches in her left foot today, and she was able
to continue dancing on her right.

As the new year begins, Palestinian resistance
attacks 5 settlements in the Galilee.

Fears of renewed tensions in crisis between
Lebanese authorities and Palestinian
resistance.

Sono Cairo Record Company presents:
Laila Nazmy's
'Spoil Your Honeymooner'.

58 per cent of Egyptians who emigrate are
engineers and highly educated;
70 per cent have a PhD.

Wagdi Phillips Co.
for new and like-new imported clothes:
English wool scarves for 15-75 piasters,
English coats, 100% wool, for 4-8 LE.

German authorities confiscate smuggled arms in
Hamburg intended for Palestinian resistance.

2 January

Egyptian Air Defence Forces down Israeli
plane near Balah.

3 January

Egyptian Special Forces unit crosses
the Suez Canal and succeeds in ambushing
Israeli patrol.

You didn't sleep that night, listening to the news. It was the War of Attrition, and you wanted to wear down the enemy, to inflict the greatest number of losses, and to raise the morale and rebuild the capabilities of the Egyptian army after the ghastly defeat of 1967, when the Israeli forces nearly made it to the outskirts of Cairo.

Every moment on the phone was a quickened heartbeat, a rush of anxiety. You were with them as they squatted in the ditches, in the destroyed village, in the abandoned fields, waiting for the signal from their companion lying at the edge of the canal with his field telephone hidden under his military coat. The silence was overpowering. The cigarettes, the racing nerves.

4

You heard him say into the phone: The first boat is now crossing the canal. And then later: The second boat is crossing. The enemy shells whistle overhead. Had they hit us? We couldn't fire back or we'd get in the way of the troops crossing. Total silence, only broken by the sound of the wind. Half an hour, then an hour. You're almost holding your breath. You look up and see your favourite photo of yourself, smiling in a silver necktie.

The crossing the night before was a complete success. One hundred soldiers complaining that the water of the canal was cold. All but three returned safely. An hour and a half. Two hours. Finally, you breathed a sigh of relief. The first and second boats were back, two wounded. The mission was complete: the explosives laid and the ambush set. Wait, stop! The scout up the Casuarina tree calls out in warning. Two tanks and a half-track carrying the enemy. Our soldiers immediately opened fire from the canal; they hit their targets. The soldier up the tree calls out again: The tanks and vehicle are destroyed! The enemy withdraws quickly. A little later two of our vehicles head back, each carrying a boat and the soldiers in their soaked clothes, half falling down from exhaustion. Their companions rush to them with bread, cheese, tea and cigarettes.

You doze off for a bit at dawn, lying on your big bed with the low wooden frame. You wake up at seven o'clock, as always. And, as always, the day begins with a shot of insulin and a bath. You shave and take the rest of your medications: for your blood pressure, your heart, your allergies, the bronchitis in your right lung. You ask yourself the same question again: Could you resign? You can only imagine yourself here at the helm, or in the grave.

You eat a simple breakfast in your bedroom—a cup of yoghurt—with your eye on the phone. You used to eat in your office on the ground floor, a breakfast of Istanbuli cheese and ful. You liked to mash the beans and mix in corn oil and lemon, and you ate the ful with cucumbers, tomatoes, arugula. You weren't allowed your usual Domiaty cheese any more because of the salt, so you were forced to eat cottage cheese, which you didn't like.

You glance at the three Cairo newspapers and then begin to get dressed. There were ten suits and eight pairs of shoes to choose from. You had two favourite pairs, the easiest on your feet. You walk several steps to the office in the adjoining room to look at the ministry reports and the telegrams from ambassadors. You sip your coffee as you read them, wishing for the cigarettes that you were not allowed to smoke. Your legs hurt. The pain from the inflamed nerves shot up your leg and into your atrophied gluteal muscles and your thighs. Your assistants move between your office and the secretary's—two floors on the other side of the street, working around the clock under the supervision of your trusted assistant Sami Sharaf (whom Sadat would send to prison in the coup of 15 May 1971, installing Ashraf Marwan in his place).

You pick up the telephone receiver and call Heikal, the masterful journalist who became your loyal friend. You'd give him what he wanted, the facts and the sources. He'd go on to write some of the most important volumes on modern Egyptian history.

A new day had begun.

4 January

Israeli armoured vehicles launch attack on southern Lebanon.

President Gamal Abdel Nasser pictured beside Anwar Sadat, who attended a Cabinet meeting for the first time in his capacity as vice president of the United Arab Republic.

You could still see the doubt in their eyes. Why him? You knew him well, or thought you did. His limited capabilities, his penchant for ostentation. The snide murmurs in your inner circle about how much he liked his own reflection. In the early days of the Revolutionary Command Council, he'd insist on having an orderly bring him ironed clothes to change into two hours into long meetings. You knew about his past in the Iron Guard—which King Farouk used to eliminate his enemies—and that he was in charge of the Kuwaiti emir's business affairs in Egypt. You'd tease him about how he was always trying to play the British gentleman, complete with pipe and hounds. It made you feel superior that you were not so easily seduced by such frivolities. You looked the other way during the many scandals—most recently, his attempt to seize Major General el-Mougy's villa. The men of the revolution had to do well, to keep them from wanting power. That had never worked with Khaled Mohieddin. You loved him but he put you on edge. He had no material desires and never slept with any woman except his wife. You always said to your men: 'Don't you want something for yourselves? Just ask.'

Whatever Sadat's failings were, he was entirely devoted to you, and had managed to convince you that he had no thirst for power, no desire to take your place. You'd never forget what he did after you returned triumphant from the Bandung Conference in 1955. Most of your colleagues addressed you by your name—he was the one who started calling you 'sir'. It was a clever signal to the others to follow suit.

You also knew that he had close ties with Kamal Adham, the director general of Saudi intelligence, who was the go-between for the Saudis and the CIA. You put up with this since a good commander kept some channels of communication with the enemy to get information and lay false trails when necessary, to help carry out your long-term plans. When Hassan al-Tuhami warned you about the plot to assassinate you in Rabat, you had to immediately decide who would stand in for you while you were away. You instantly thought of Sadat. He was the only one left from the Revolutionary Council. The others were under-standably embittered by the defeat of 1967. Sadat was one of the few who had stayed by your side after the whole ordeal. His home was a welcome refuge and his wife had a knack for hosting dinners that soothed your pent-up nerves. Sadat himself would cook for you sometimes, always asking after your health and regaling you with the latest popular jokes from the hashish dens.

When Zakaria Mohieddin resigned as vice president in March 1968 and disappeared from public life, Sadat was next in line based on seniority and the sacred hierarchy of military cohort, to which you were always faithful. Sadat was more senior than Hussein al-Shafei in the Revolutionary Council. Al-Shafei was scrupulous, courageous and devout. He had been success-ful in the sectors he oversaw—but less so in the Socialist Union.

He'd been the first secretary general from 1962 to 1965 but lacked a certain poise and skill.

There were all kinds of other things to take into account too, including dealing with the Soviets who had refused to support the Egyptian Air Defence Forces because they were uncertain of the fitness of the army, and were afraid of a repeat of the debacle of 1967. They were also afraid of winding up in direct confrontation with the US. And there was the matter of placating King Faisal, since Sadat had developed close ties with Kamal Adham, Faisal's brother-in-law, after a dinner hosted by musician and actor Farid al-Atrash, which resulted in Adham paying Sadat a monthly sum. Leadership was a difficult business.

That was why you turned a blind eye to what happened in 1966. At the beginning of the year Sadat was invited by the US ambassador to visit Washington with the International Visitors Program under the auspices of the State Department. There was a CIA agent beside him the whole trip. Sadat and his wife spent ten days in the US. It later became clear that the trip was orchestrated by Kamal Adham. During Sadat's trip to Washington, he met with the Kuwaiti emir, Sheikh Mubarak Al Sabah, and implied that his official travel compensation was less than it ought to be. The emir wrote him a cheque for 35,000 dollars. When you got wind of this, you asked Sadat what had happened and asked him to personally return the sum to the emir (though later it turned out that he never did).

Who else, then? You were diametrically opposed to picking someone outside the military order of cohort and rank and choosing any old civilian. You thought they were spineless, unfit to lead; this was the domain of the military alone, those who were trained to listen and obey. There were some civilians who'd done well—Aziz Sedky, Labib Shuqair, Diaa al-Din Dawoud, even Sedki Sulayman. And Heikal—Heikal was the best of them. He was by your side in everything. But you'd never leave the keys of the army and security to any of them.

The circle was getting increasingly small. Ali Sabri? There was only one mark against him: He didn't have much of a following. He wasn't well-liked in right-wing and conservative circles. And you had a bad feeling about his thirst for power. You'd laugh at how he always tried to overtake Sadat—they'd speed to see who could pull up first at meetings or who could stand closer to you in front of the camera.

So who was left? There was Kamal Rifaat, one of the Free Officers and your match in poise and diligence. But he was too close to Abdel Hakim Amer and had married a former dancer. There was also Tharwat Okasha, who had been there from the beginning, but you knew about his escapades with women and that he was close to the corrupt head of intelligence, Salah Nasr.

That was it, then. Anwar Sadat was more or less the only one who had never stood against you.

You could have chosen al-Tuhami from the military ranks but he had a rather murky past. He had been one of the first Free Officers and was with you in the siege of al-Faluja in Palestine. He'd been with Sadat in the king's Iron Guard and worked alongside him in the Islamic Congress of Egypt, Saudi Arabia and Pakistan, which was formed in 1954.

Al-Tuhami was a peculiar and devout fellow. He'd eventually become a dervish and was convinced he was clairvoyant. He'd be sitting among his colleagues and then suddenly spring up and proclaim, 'And greetings to you too!' and inform everyone that Sayyiduna al-Khidr had just passed through and said hello, but that the Verdant One could only be seen with the second sight.

When the Cairo Tower was being built—with money from the Americans who were trying to buy you out—he took over the first floor and made it his private fortress. Later it came out you'd had him eavesdrop on the telephone conversations of members of the Revolutionary Council and the ministers. While he was on missions abroad, he rose to pray at dawn and at other times throughout the day and night, and would throw open the windows and make the call to prayer in a thunderous voice that would attract the attention of foreign security forces. You summoned him back to Egypt and put him in charge of overseeing the presidential palace after the defeat of 1967, to protect you from wiretapping, explosives, poison gas, tainted food or whatever else the Americans might devise. In May of the following year, the Egyptian intelligence warned you that there were signs that Hassan al-Tuhami was himself working for the CIA and that he was recording important state phone calls. But you brushed this aside—things were awry in your intelligence, anyway—and gave him a ministerial post in your last government, where everyone applauded his industriousness, piety and integrity. He kept having spiritual experiences, like a number of others after the defeat. Your men were all visiting fortune-tellers and soothsayers. Those beliefs even resonated with earlier parts of your own life, despite your rationality and unshakeable belief in science.

You were inclined to believe al-Tuhami when he went to Morocco with the delegation for the Arab League summit in Rabat, and sent you a telegram warning you that General Oufkir was plotting to kill you. That was when you decided to appoint a deputy. The only option was Sadat. Al-Tuhami had alluded before that he had seen you and Sadat in one of his visions, going together to meet the Holy Prophet. Afterwards it turned out that there was no Oufkir conspiracy.

Those two—Sadat and al-Tuhami—were the ones who pointed out the capable young Air Force officer Hosni Mubarak, who later became a major arms dealer with close ties to the Western intelligence agencies. Several years later, on 22 February 1977, the prominent US investigative journalist Jim Hoagland wrote an article in *The Washington Post* detailing Sadat and Kamal Adham's ties to the CIA.

6 January

Egyptian forces cross the Suez Canal and clash
with the Israeli enemy for 3 hours.

Air Defence Forces down Israeli plane over
the canal.

Marxism and modern philosophy removed from
Egyptian schoolbooks.

Cartoon by Salah Jahin:
If kids want to understand Marxism,
they should go to the American University of
Cairo—they teach that there.

Al-Ahram:
Some Arab nationalist forces continue to forget
Israel and instead wage holy war on communism.

The Daily Telegraph:
Israel is the best and most durable ally for
the West.

Recent attempts to provoke the Lebanese
government against the Palestinian resistance.

7 January

Series of Israeli airstrikes in the Egyptian
interior utilize the latest US planes.

8 January

General Emile Boustany removed as commander of the
Lebanese armed forces and Major General Jean
Njaim, known for his hostility towards the
Palestinian resistance, appointed in his place.

Tenth anniversary of the Aswan High Dam.

What to watch: Top TV series.

In most recent cabinet reshuffle in Iraq,
communist minister chosen for the first time since
Abd al-Karim Qasim's rule came to an end in 1963.
Ba'ath Party takes full control of legislative and
executive powers. Legislative authority now rests
with the Revolutionary Command Council while
executive power is in the hands of Hassan al-Bakr,
the party's secretary general.

French youth hijacks US plane and diverts the
flight to Beirut, intending to hand over the
passengers as hostages in Lebanon in exchange for
19 Lebanese persons kidnapped by Israeli forces in
attacks on southern Lebanon.

285,000 imported blankets in Egyptian markets
Polish blankets: 275 piasters.

The Egyptian General Cinema Foundation's
new line-up for the new year:

Majnun Layla by Tharwat Abaza, screenplay by
Youssef Francis, directed by Kamal El Sheikh.

Return of the Spirit by Tawfiq al-Hakim,
screenplay by Ali el-Zorkani, directed by
Salah Abu Seif.

Back Streets by Abdel Rahman al-Sharqawi,
directed by Kamal Attia.

The Days by Taha Hussein, screenplay by
Hassan Fouad, directed by Tewfik Saleh.

The Mirage by Naguib Mahfouz, directed by Atef Salem.

A Nose and Three Eyes by Ihsan Abdel Quddous.

The Choice, screenplay by Naguib Mahfouz,
directed by Youssef Chahine.

The Voice of Islam by Ali Ahmad Bakathir.

The White Sail by Abdel Moneim el-Sawy.

At six o'clock in the evening you met the three journalists in your office. They were from three different Lebanese newspapers— one funded by the Saudis, one by the British intelligence, and the third by the Egyptian embassy. You'd insisted on meeting with them together.

You said that you had never thought of war as a solution to the Arab–Israeli conflict. In your opinion, there were other ways to outdo them. Israel was just an arm of US imperialism which wanted to control the Middle East's oil and resources, and the real battle was against those US schemes. But Israel wanted war and had amassed its forces at the Syrian border. They knew that you'd be forced to come to Syria's aid. Everything had been expertly arranged. We fell into the trap that had been so carefully set, and now it was on us to liberate our land.

You said to them, 'War has destroyed a great deal of our country. It has destroyed the Suez and Ismailia. We relocated almost 400,000 Egyptians from the canal area to the interior. We halted production in all the industrial plants there. We gave each family a salary and subsidized their rent . . . 110 million pounds gone, and then we lost the oil! We closed the refineries and started importing refined petroleum instead, which costs twice as much as crude oil. We had three refineries, and fertilizer from our own factories—enough fertilizer to meet half the country's needs. And we had other factories—for paper, paint, televisions, lightbulbs. All of these have closed.'

It was painful for you to sit during the speech and to stand afterwards for the photos. You met with some of the leaders of the Socialist Union's Vanguard Organization. They quickly asked the usual question, 'When are we going to war?' You answered, 'Well, we're not, not tomorrow, or the day after tomorrow or next month. If Israel's planes attack, we still can't go to war in 1970, for a simple reason—I have 400 planes, but I don't have 400 pilots. Training pilots takes a year and a half. They get their pilots from the US and France and South Africa! So their problem is solved. Each Phantom needs two pilots— 50 Phantoms require 100 pilots.'

You talked a lot. You loved to talk and often wore out the people listening. You exhausted people at meetings as you reeled off facts and dates. At this time of day you were at your best and most focused—the later it got, the more animated you became, the more tightly wound your nerves. The whole time you never stopped drinking coffee—sometimes you drank twenty cups in an evening. Or smoking, until you at last gave that up on doctor's orders.

You answered many questions. You said that socialism would liberate humanity from economic and social exploitation: 'We are in a transitional stage from capitalism to socialism . . . that doesn't mean we're going to nationalize a few factories and have done with it. No—socialism means we build a just society. The residue of the old system lingers on, of the old feudal and capitalist networks. That class is still here and will take decades to die out. People are by nature conservative and holding property is a human instinct. If you want to enact change in this system of ownership, you're not only up against the natural instincts of everyone affected by these changes, you're also dealing with all those who are not big landowners right now but dream of becoming one someday. During this phase, you're transitioning from a society ruled by the few to a society with just distribution of resources. This is an incredibly difficult process. This transitional period is the most perilous for societies because the old structures have collapsed, but the new have not yet come to be.'

Then you explained the theory of surplus value—the cornerstone of Marxist thought—and the nature of capitalist exploitation. You told them that you had previously believed that socialism would be achieved through the people taking control of the means of production as set forth in the National Charter, but now you understood it would be achieved through the people owning the means of production.

One of them asked you, 'Will this apply to all units of production regardless of size?'

You responded in the affirmative: 'Yes, if the unit has any workers at all, otherwise it will become a site for the exploitation of brother by brother.' You gave the example of your uncle who made 600 LE a month from hiring drivers for his three trucks while he sat in an office making money off their sweat.

Another asked, 'Is a mechanic who owns a small workshop and has two apprentices going to be subject to the same policy?'

You said, 'Yes, I think so. Or he needs to let them have an equal share of the profits.'

You looked at them, scrutinized their faces. You knew you were treading in dangerous waters. You had previously expressed these ideas to your longtime colleagues—Abdel Hakim Amer, Anwar Sadat, al-Shafei, al-Boghdadi, Zakaria Mohieddin and Kamal el-Din Hussein—back in March 1964. At the time some of them were speechless, while others voiced their displeasure. Kamal el-Din Hussein cried out, 'In your dreams!' He had spoken before about how important it was for our socialism to be grounded in Islam.

Very few of the men in the Socialist Union were receptive to the idea. Most of them just looked at you in apprehensive silence. Your frustration was cut short by the arrival of the first edition of the gazette published by the State Information Service—one hundred copies for you and the other top officials, containing international newspapers, bulletins and broadcasts, books that had been recently published, and a twenty-page summary on the most important new writers from around the world.

The Socialist Union men seized the opportunity to take their leave.

11 January

Egyptian planes destroy largest Israeli missile
base in the Gulf of Suez.

Ezer Weizman, Israeli minister of transportation:
I support the full political and economic
integration of the areas that Israel occupied in
the June War.

13 January

Israel asks US for more Phantom planes.

Golda Meir: No chance of peace in the Middle East
while Abdel Nasser remains in power.

'Men are the Protectors':
Celebration held aboard the *Goddess Isis* featuring a
two-metre-high wedding cake. President Abdel Nasser's
secretary Mohamed Ahmed, Abdel Magid Farid and Abdel
Hamid al-Sarraj offered their congratulations to the
couple. Suddenly the father of the bride appeared—
Farouq Aqil, managing director of the al-Ahlia
Insurance Company and vice president of Tersana
Sporting Club. He tried to conceal the small box he
was carrying in his hand and everyone wanted to know
what was inside. A fight broke out between the father
of the bride and some of the high-profile guests, to
the amusement of all. Finally, it was revealed to the
attendees that the box contained a gold chain with
the Qur'anic verse: 'Men are the protectors of
women.' The male guests applauded loudly and the
women objected even louder.

Rabso: Effortless cleaning.

Ideal fulfils the dream of every family for a streamlined kitchen in attractive colours. Plain kitchen for 34 LE and in colour for 38 LE, or in instalments: 2 LE per month (plain) and 2.50 LE per month (colour) for 15 months.

Abdel Wahab el-Beshry, minister of military production, visits factories belonging to El Nasr Company for Transformers and Electrical Products (ELMACO).

Mohamed Abdel Aziz, the clothing designer on Qasr El Nil Street, travels abroad to see the latest fashions and clothing styles for men.

IDF magazine *Ma'arachot* reports that Egypt has received 2 billion dollars' worth of weapons from the Soviet Union since the June 1967 War.

23 ships secretly ferry US arms to Israel from Belgium's Zeebrugge port.

Israeli planes repelled after attempting to strike Tell El Kebir.

Second anniversary of the passing of
Wing Commander Labib Fanous.
First anniversary of the passing of
Major Fathallah Zayed.
Second anniversary of the passing of
Air Commodore Mohamed Amin Ayoub.
First anniversary of the passing of
Major Mohamed Mousa Mohamed.

15 January

Abdel Nasser's fifty-second birthday.

You stood up with great effort. The pain in your legs was excruciating. You went to the bathroom to wash and stood looking at yourself in the mirror: White hair advancing on both sides. Your piercing eyes with that strange mix of grey and green, which transfixed anyone looking into them. But today they were weary, clouded by exhaustion. You thought of the dangers before you, and the conversation your intelligence agency had recorded between an Israeli and US official in the US embassy in Cairo. They had decided it would be necessary to use either poison or illness to get rid of you.

You put on a Stia suit, which you were proud of because it was made in the UAR. The children were making less of a racket today because of their mother. Your birthday had become children's day. Was that ironic? Hardly. Hadn't you given the country something entirely new? You were serious (weren't you?) when you yelled, the day of the assassination attempt in al-Manshiya: 'Didn't I teach you any self-respect?'

Suddenly your eyes filled with tears as they always did when you remembered her. Your mother . . . a wound that would never heal. The girl your father married when he worked as a coal porter for a well-known merchant in the Bakos neighbourhood of Alexandria, in addition to his main job as a postal clerk. He summoned the courage, backed up by his job at the post office, to propose to the merchant's daughter Fahima. You were her first child. Your father worked morning till night for 7 or 8 pounds, which meant your mother and her eldest son spent a lot of time together, without any rival for her attention and care.

Then the family moved to Khatatba when your father was transferred to the post office there, even though you still attended the primary school in Alexandria. In Khatatba you had your first lessons in social class. Not far away was the estate of Mubarak Bey al-Gayar, and you often went there with your father and rode the Bey's donkey. You became friends with his son, who later became one of your aides. There you became acquainted with the wretched lives of the fellahin and the complacent power of the landowners.

During this period, you saw less of your mother, whom you adored—just hurried visits and letters in the mail, until that fateful day when you were eight years old. When the school holidays started, you went to the house in Khatatba and found a lady living there named Enayyat al-Sahn, not Fahima Hammad, who you were told had died a while ago after the birth of your brother Shawky. No one had told you. It was the first of many blows in your life.

You wiped away your tears as you came out of the bathroom. It was painful to walk downstairs to the ground floor which had now been fully secured against both wiretapping and explosives. Everyone was waiting for you to go to al-Qanatir al-Khayriyya just outside Cairo, where the government had built a three-storey rest house back in King Farouk's day that had been used by the prime minister for several years. You went in your car, which was just like your office. You had your papers, your secretary, your telephone that never stopped ringing. You followed the news from the front minute by minute. That was how you spent the vacation.

You still found some time in the evenings to spend with your family. You told them, laughing, about Muammar Gaddafi's antics at the Rabat summit several weeks ago. That must have been the first official summit he had attended—less than four months after the military coup that brought him to power. He was a young man who didn't know anything about international protocol. Just like you in 1952.

Before the summit began, the chief of the Moroccan royal court arrived and told King Hassan II that the hall was ready and took the king's outstretched hand and kissed it. Gaddafi was taken aback and cried out, 'What is this? Kissing hands? Are we back in the era of slavery again? No! This is unacceptable.'

That wasn't the only time Gaddafi ruffled everyone's feathers at the summit. He also addressed the Moroccan king as 'Hassan' and got into a spat with King Faisal Al Saud in which he flung his pistol down on the table. At that the Saudi king got up to leave, protesting about dealings with guns, until you and King Hassan II intervened and convinced him not to go. But Gaddafi kept getting into trouble even after the meeting ended. When General Mohamed Oufkir, the Moroccan minister of the interior, came into the hall, Gaddafi began to shout, 'Arrest this man! What is he doing here? He's a murderer.' (That was because Oufkir had been accused of assassinating the Moroccan opposition leader Mehdi Ben Barka.) 'He belongs in prison, not here!'

Tensions reached a breaking point when Gaddafi began his retort to King Faisal with 'Well, Faisal,' without the slightest hint of decorum. The Saudi monarch left the conference hall for good and King Hassan II had to adjourn the session so everyone could cool off.

In the end, because of the tussles during those last meetings, the Iraqi, Syrian and Yemeni delegations didn't show up to the final session. You declared the summit a failure and said that you too would be forced to leave.

You told your family about how it later turned out that King Hassan II had given the Israeli Mossad a special room adjacent to the summit meetings from which they listened to the failed conference and recorded the discussions.

You wanted to lighten the mood after that, so you told them some of Sadat's favourite jokes: 'There was once a man who was out of work. He went and caught a fish and ran back home to tell his wife, but she said they had no oil to fry the fish. The man said, "Well, boil it then." She replied, "But there is no gas for the stove." So the man took the fish and threw it back in the sea. As soon as it hit the water, the fish raised its head and cried, "Long live Abdel Nasser!"'

Then you told another joke that they seemed to have heard before: 'A fat dog ran away from Egypt to Libya. All the skinny dogs there asked him, "What are you doing here? We've got nothing to eat." And he said, "I'm here just to bark!"' That led to countless other jokes.

You said to the children that the whole world was trying to keep youth out of politics and distracted with sports and new kinds of dancing, and that was very dangerous.

For a moment, you lost your train of thought. Then you told the story of how when you applied to the Military Academy for the first time, they had wanted to know: Is your father a big shot? Have you got an army officer in your family? Does your family own land? Is there someone recommending you? When you replied no to all the questions, they said, 'Well, what are you doing trying to become an officer, then?' That gave you a new understanding of how social class worked.

The family had brought you gifts: Rivoli slippers, a scissors case, two Hussein Genedi button-up shirts. You said as you opened them, 'When I was a kid, I didn't get to have a birthday.'

The whole family returned to Cairo that evening without you for the birthday celebrations in Manshiyat al-Bakri and blew out your candles, while you stayed in al-Qanatir for two more days. You didn't join in the rest of the festivities. They didn't know you wouldn't celebrate another birthday after that.

Just out from *al-Ahram*'s Dar al-Kitab al-Jadid:
At the Mercy of the Fates.

Vice President Sadat at Cairo University:
The next six months will determine the outcome of
the battle.

Film: *A Man for All Seasons.*

Lebanese security orders members of the
Palestinian resistance to abandon their positions.

Israeli artillery strikes the village of Yarine in
southern Lebanon.

New short story by Lotfy El Kholy:
'The Man Who Saw the Sole of His Left Foot in a
Broken Mirror'.

He is survived by a brother, the director general
of the Ministry of Planning; nephews and nieces,
including the managing editor of a daily
newspaper, a student in the *lycée,* the wife of a
major in the police force, and the wife of the
director of the Suez Canal Authority; cousins,
including the governor of Cairo during the
monarchy, a major general in the armed forces, the

president of Misr Cotton Company, the director of
the National Bank of Egypt, and an advisor to the
State Council; and siblings, including a radio
producer, a teacher in Saudi Arabia and a lawyer
for the State Information Service.

Funeral services held for
Lieutenant Colonel Labib Zaki Habib.

Lawyer Ahmed Hussein, founder of the Young Egypt
Party, flies to London to continue treatment at
the expense of the Egyptian state.

Your political journey began with him. After the shock of your
mother's death, the shock of finding another woman living in
the house, you asked your father to let you live with your grandfather in Alexandria. You wanted to be free from your father's
unrelenting severity, which melted away with the children of his
second wife. You started at Ras El Tin Secondary School and fell
in love with reading, especially about great leaders: Napoleon,
Alexander the Great, Ataturk. You loved Tawfiq al-Hakim's novel,
Return of the Spirit, and you underlined the part about how
Egyptians were missing a true commander to rally around. You
began to imagine yourself as that leader, the one that Egypt and
the Arab world had been waiting for.

One evening in July 1934, when you were fifteen or sixteen,
you were walking through the streets of Alexandria and saw a
crowd of people heading towards Muhammad Ali Square. You
followed them without realizing what was going on, and when
you got to the square there were people giving speeches and
protestors chanting against the British occupation. The British
policemen and soldiers fired several times at the protestors. You

chanted against the British, calling for them to leave Egypt. They arrested you with dozens of other protestors and took everyone into custody at the al-Manshiya police station. There you learned that the demonstration had been organized by the Young Egypt Party in response to the British crackdown on another protest in Mansoura. In the morning the neighbourhood sheikh came and you were released.

Once you were out you wanted to learn more about the Young Egypt Party. You got to know Ahmed Hussein and his colleague Fathi Radwan. Their platform caught your attention and you joined. When you moved to Cairo, you settled in al-Zaher near the Young Egypt Party headquarters. The party journal, *al-Sarkha*, was printed by al-Raghaib Press behind Cinema Royal. You'd bring the copies from the press to the headquarters and use the few piasters you had on you to buy postage stamps so the journal could be sent out to subscribers. Then you'd take the copies to the post office in Attaba and mail them. In the end you'd be left without a single penny so you'd have to return to al-Zaher on foot. That journey back was always perilous—you were arrested several times.

Not long after you parted ways and were drawn to other political movements like the Muslim Brotherhood and the communists. Ahmed Hussein was not much of a leader. He was a firebrand with little guiding him beyond some impassioned nationalist slogans. Still, he'd played a key part in the run-up to the revolution. You were both in the Free Officers and used to distribute its paper *al-Ishtirakiya*, with bold red headlines announcing the king's corruption scandals and calling for revolution. After the Cairo Fire, the king took revenge on Ahmed Hussein and he was tried on charges of instigating the fire and sentenced to death. The only thing that could save him from the gallows was a military coup. Even then you kept him in prison for three months out of fear of his popular following and his ability to stir people up. You took an interest in his closest associate, Fathi Radwan, who was not released until his moment had passed. He'd decide he wanted to retire from political life and devoted himself to writing instead. Shortly afterwards Radwan was struck by polio, although that didn't stop him from penning a singular encyclopedia on Egyptian history, parts of which he wrote from bed.

16 January

Egyptian Air Defence Forces down 3 Skyhawk planes on the canal front.

Central Bank of Egypt receives monthly aid package from Kuwaiti government worth 3.25 million LE.

17 January

Silent march of Palestinian organizations in Amman.

President Abdel Nasser performed the Eid prayer yesterday morning after recovering from a bad flu that had kept him on bedrest for a week.

That was the phrasing that Heikal had suggested for your heart attack. It was the second time. The first time had been the year before and afterwards they installed the lift so you wouldn't have to take the stairs. You didn't leave your bedroom and spent all day on the phone with the army command and ministers, getting the news from the front and giving your directives. You ate light meals with your wife in the same room. Before, you'd usually eat with the whole family in a room where the children's crayon scribblings covered the walls and door. Now you spent your days between the bed and the armchair beside it, looking out the window into the back garden for long periods of time. You used to watch your son Khalid out there when he was in school as he pretended to give speeches, imitating you.

Less than two weeks later you began seeing visitors again in the little office adjoining your bedroom. A month later, you used the lift for the first time and went down to your main office.

You began this journey with illness in 1958—after the Suez war and the plot against Syria, after the United Arab Republic was formed, after the revolution and fall of the Baghdad Pact in Iraq. That was when your doctors discovered the diabetes. It was hereditary on your father's side and they said you would need to adjust your diet, avoid overexertion and minimize sources of agitation. The first of these was reasonable—with the exception of white cheese—but the other two were impossible.

Everything happened quickly in Iraq and spiralled out of your control. You had wanted to impose your unfortunate take on democracy—which did away with every political entity except you—on a noble people with a long-standing political struggle and well-established political parties. The enemy took advantage of your narcissism and you fell into the trap. As usual, you threw yourself into a pointless fight with the communists. Then you ran into problems with the union with Syria and with your old colleagues from the Revolutionary Command Council. The next blow was the unravelling of the union with Syria and its aftershocks in Egypt and throughout the Arab world. Then came the war in Yemen; your development plans, one after the next, each with its triumphs and difficulties; the fears of disloyalty from within; and finally the defeat of 1967 and those two enervating days—9 and 10 June.

During all this, the diabetes was getting worse. When they ran the tests on 13 July, it showed that the disease had affected the arteries in your right foot.

You buried yourself in the process of rebuilding the armed forces and reforming the ranks on the home front and on the Arab front, as if punishing yourself for the defeat.

On the plane to Moscow in July 1968, the pain was so intense that you couldn't sit down, so the doctors made up a bed for you in your private section at the front of the plane. Yasser Arafat was on that plane to Moscow, travelling as a technical advisor under the name Amin. No one knew he was on the plane and no one had heard of him yet anyway. You had taken him with you to Moscow to give the Palestinian resistance a potential arms source. You asked him to sit beside you, and by the time he did, you had gained full control over the pain. He could not see it written on your face.

You managed to maintain full composure as you went through the ordeal of arriving at the airport in Russia. You endured the official welcome standing upright on your feet until you reached the guesthouse atop the Lenin Hills. Then you had a preliminary meeting with the Soviet leaders and a friendly chat with them while walking in the gardens, where Brezhnev showed you the cherry trees. Finally you went up to your bedroom, took off your clothes and stretched out on the bed. Your private doctor came and you went to the Barvikha sanitorium, where you underwent a full examination and they found atherosclerosis in the arteries in your leg. They asked you to quit smoking for good.

You put out your last cigarette. That was it—the only luxury in your life, gone. By the spring and summer of 1969 the artillery battles had begun. You followed the dangerous operations across the canal night after night, hearing the name of each troop's leader as they went in, asking about the losses they'd incurred. You declared a war of attrition in July and the fighting heated up on the Egyptian front. In the middle of all this, you were supposed to take your second trip to Tskaltubo to finally get rid of the pain, but you postponed the trip until September, until after the political situation had settled. The pain became more acute again, until you could hardly stand it.

The pain was unbearable if you walked for more than ten minutes or if you sat in place for more than an hour. But even this could not extinguish your good cheer, your perennial capacity to see the bright side of everything.

Then came 10 September 1969.

At 9 a.m. you were watching the training exercises near the Cairo–Suez highway when all of a sudden dispatches started coming in about an Israeli landing operation in the Zaafarana area of the Gulf of Suez. The reports out of Tel Aviv and other major cities around the world were saying that there had been an attempted invasion of Egypt. Some new outlets claimed to be reporting from 'occupied Egypt'. You ordered the armed forces to be on call and at the ready.

You returned to Cairo two hours later and began to sift through the reports and figure out what was happening. By 5 p.m. it was becoming clear that the objective of the Israeli operation was psychological, because they had withdrawn their forces by nightfall.

You were set to travel to Tskaltubo only a few days later.

The next day you felt exhausted and dizzy. The doctors said it was a heart attack and prescribed three weeks' bedrest. You called Heikal to your bedroom to get his advice on the matter. When you asked him what could be said about this three-week absence so that the country wouldn't worry, he suggested the story about the flu.

That night there was a crisis between the Jordanian government and the Palestinian resistance. King Hussein sent Prime Minister Bahjat Talhouni to Cairo with a message for you. Talhouni asked to meet with you because the situation had become dire. He was told that the president was suffering from a bout of influenza and was on bedrest. Talhouni seemed to want to find out if you were still alive and declared that his government would resign if he returned home without seeing you. A compromise was reached: Talhouni was allowed to come up to your bedroom and see you, provided he did not bother you about anything. This way he could say to the king that he had met with you, but actually get what he wanted from Vice President Anwar Sadat.

No one knew what had happened. Even your wife didn't suspect anything until they started working on the lift.

A secret urgent message was sent to Moscow and Dr Chazov, a leading cardiologist and Soviet minister of health, came to visit you.

He ran his tests and got the same results.

You said to him, 'I was supposed to go to Tskaltubo, to finish the treatment for the arteritis.'

Chazov said, 'Sir, that is no longer possible, because your heart cannot tolerate mineral water treatment now. You'll have to wait at least five years for that.'

You thought again of stepping down. Not for yourself, for the country. You could explain that you had fallen into despair after the war, which would cast a shadow over the armed forces and the Arab people.

You thought: Could a new organization be put together to relieve you of some of the work? But you could see that was not possible. Every delegation that arrived wanted to talk with you. You had to make an appearance at every public occasion. Everything related to the war you had to decide yourself. That was the crux of the matter: If it was not in your hands, you would no longer exist.

That was how you convinced yourself.

You kept your feet but it was one thing after the next: The Arab League summit in Rabat and then your first trip to Libya, when you stood in a Jeep in Benghazi for four long hours, weaving through a sea of people. You came back to Egypt with a bad flu—a real flu this time—and had to rest for a while.

3 Israeli Skyhawks downed over Gulf of Suez:
A grand moment for the Egyptian Air Defence
Forces.

You'd been waiting for news since two o'clock. Your heart was pounding. We shot down the first plane at 2.20 p.m. The Israeli airstrikes on Egypt were expected to reach up to forty-two strikes per day. Until that point, Egypt's success in fortifying its air defence on the front had been limited. The enemy had the newest American technologies and could track Egyptian movements at lightning speed. There would have to be a third attempt to bring in the new Soviet anti-aircraft missiles for the Air Defence Forces. You set the day for the operation, but you felt uneasy when you thought about some of the things that had happened recently. Just before zero hour you had an odd premonition to delay. Strangely enough, there was an unprecedented wave of airstrikes at the front that night—it was as if they knew. So you had been right: Someone was leaking our secrets. But who? You called to mind the names of those who had known about the plan. You'd had suspicions for a while, but all your many security agencies had failed to identify this internal foe. Should you form a new security apparatus, then?

18 January

King Faisal returns to Riyadh after 3 weeks of medical tests in France, followed by 4 days in Switzerland.

Revolution before development, or development before revolution?

Third Development Plan to target heavy and medium industry instead of light and consumer industries.

19 January

Egyptian forces destroy Israeli frogmen attempting to cross the canal.

Pravda:
Hundreds of thousands of Arabs in the Occupied Territories forcibly expelled from their homes; Israelis destroy 7,000 houses.

Lebanese minister Pierre Gemayel demands that Palestinian refugees in Lebanon be redistributed among Arab countries.

Thirty-Sixth Annual Conference of the Academy of Arabic Language headed by Dr Taha Hussein begins in Cairo.

In Egyptian hospitals, only 15 piasters are allocated per patient for daily meals. The tragedy spans requisition fiascos to kitchens run in the most primitive way, lacking even serving dishes. In most of the 179 public and central hospitals and 578 health clinics, a private contractor oversees the food supply orders. Some use subcontractors to carry out the work. These contractors employ countless methods to snatch procurement opportunities from public sector companies. Some provide huge quantities of certain food items that do not match the hospital's specifications. If the delivery is refused, a petty fine is imposed. The hospital can then buy what it needs from the market, while the contractor still makes a profit in the end.

21 January

Palestinian resistance forces shell Israeli potash factories for the second time, halting production.

Resistance operations escalate in Gaza and the Jordan Valley.

Abba Eban: Abdel Nasser is the no.1 enemy of Israel.

22 Iraqis executed for plotting against the
regime, including 18 soldiers; total of 40 Iraqis
executed in the same case.

Production at Helwan complex for civil and war
industries (with 20,000 skilled workers) rises to
5 million LE by year end.

22 January

Secret visit by President Abdel Nasser to the
Soviet Union lasts 4 days.

You asked them for surface-to-air missiles to use against the low-altitude Israeli aircraft. This was difficult since the SA-3 had not previously been used outside the Soviet Union. After some discussion they agreed to send Egypt the new anti-aircraft system within twenty days. But Egyptian forces would require a further six months to learn to use the new system, so you also asked for Soviet experts to help operate the system until the Egyptian forces were able to do so.

That was an even more difficult request, because it was the first time that the Soviets had done that kind of thing. As Kosygin said to you, 'This could lead to a confrontation with the US.' Brezhnev added, 'The anti-aircraft system will need air cover, so if we are talking about sending these missiles, we are also talking about sending air force units at the same time.'

You agreed to the Soviet Union sending air force units to protect the SA-3 missile system. But Brezhnev insisted that the US would see that as a military threat.

They asked to have until the next day to consult further on the matter.

The Guardian:
Israelis hope for a change in Egypt's leadership.

Israeli intelligence behind
explosions in Lebanon.

Radio Baghdad interrupts its broadcast to announce that a plot to bring down the government with the aid of foreign agents has been foiled. Mohammed Saeed al-Sahhaf, director-general of radio and television, made the announcement. He stated that a 'group of traitors' had tried to undermine the immortal 17 July Revolution—a progressive popular movement that has overcome the scourges of colonialism, Zionism and subjugation.

Egyptian National Assembly proposes price cap of 55 piasters per kilo for red meat.

Libyan Air Force assumes control of Tajura, a key US military intelligence facility with radio communications to NATO bases in Western Europe and West Asia. This marks the end of the second stage of turning over the enormous Wheelus Air Base to the new Libyan government.

Second anniversary of the passing of
First Lieutenant Rashid Hassan.

Execution of twelve Iraqis on charges of conspiracy: Twelve Iraqis were executed yesterday afternoon after being tried before a special military tribunal for conspiring to overthrow the Iraqi regime in collaboration with foreign agents. The

special tribunal began at 2 p.m., approximately an
hour and a half after the Revolutionary Command
Council made the announcement. The special
tribunal issued a statement that the executions of
the first group, which included five military
personnel, had taken place at 4.30 p.m.
The second group, which included six military
personnel and one civilian, was executed
shortly after. The statement indicated that the
conspirators had aimed to dismantle the 17 July
Revolution and return Iraq 'to the reactionary age
of feudalism and exploitation, and to prevent it
from accomplishing its noble mission to
free Palestine'.

Saudi Arabia pays its share of aid instalments to
the UAR totalling 10.25 million LE for the fight
against the enemy.

That was one of the achievements of the Arab League summit of 1967, held in Khartoum two months after the defeat. Without the aid from the summit, Egypt would really have suffered by the end of that year. Your plane had landed at the Khartoum airport at the same time as King Faisal's and the master of ceremonies asked whether you'd mind coming out with the king in the same car. You had the presence of mind to tell him absolutely not. That was the right choice—no sooner had your car left the airport than crowds of hundreds of thousands who had been waiting for hours in the suffocating heat and humidity began to chant: Nasser! Nasser!

Faisal would have shared this welcome with you in Khartoum, but you deprived him of that opportunity. The crowds' chants lifted your spirits even as seeing Faisal dampened them.

During the proceedings with the other Arab leaders, King Faisal kept repeating: Long may you live. You smiled bitterly because you knew full well that he wanted the opposite. His previous dealings with you were evidence of that. In 1962, when he was crown prince, he went to Washington to plead for aid to confront the threat you posed to reactionary regimes in the region. The US provided air cover, and then he brought in thousands of European mercenaries and Yemeni royalists who supported the deposed King al-Badr. The CIA and British intelligence got involved, as well as King Hussein, Haile Selassie (the emperor of Ethiopia), the Iranian Shah's intelligence, Pakistani intelligence and Mossad. Robert Komer, who was in charge of Middle Eastern affairs for the US National Security Council, oversaw the operation. Faisal funded and armed a Brotherhood group with help from the Saudi and Sudanese Brotherhood, including Hassan al-Turabi and Sadiq Abdul Majid. He also coordinated with Said Ramadan and others who were working with Western intelligence agencies to try to bring down your regime through assassination attempts and other attacks.

You tried several times to end the war in Yemen and to work with the Saudis to reach a political solution to the conflict. Your last attempt to negotiate peace was in August 1965.

By 1965, the US had evidently decided to do away with you and your regime. They had Faisal set up the Islamic Alliance to counter the ideological appeal of secular Arab nationalism. They also cut wheat aid to escalate economic pressure on Egypt.

By 1967, most of the stars of the global liberation and non-aligned movements had been extinguished: Sukarno in Indonesia, Nkrumah in Ghana, Ben Bella in Algeria, Ben Barka in Morocco, Papandreou in Greece. Faisal had been informed by his head of intelligence and brother-in-law Kamal Adham that a secret military organization led by Group Captain Daoud al-Tawwil was poised to carry out a coup against the Saudi ruling family in June 1969. The conspirators were executed by being thrown out of planes in the Empty Quarter, after some had confessed under brutal torture to having ties with your aide Sami Sharaf. In 1967, Faisal had figured that your time was up. But by some miracle, you were still standing.

So what was he playing at now?

23 January

That morning there was a decisive meeting with the Soviet leadership. You suspected, based on previous experience, that there was some kind of tussle going on behind the scenes between the three top leaders. It transpired that the Arab–Israeli conflict was at the core of this dispute. You could see from their body language that Brezhnev was going to win that battle. Podgorny, the head of the state, said, 'What you are asking is for us to get involved in a war, and that is incredibly risky.' Kosygin, the premier, echoed him, as did Brezhnev, the general secretary of the communist party.

You took another gamble and said, 'Well, why don't we just let the US do whatever it likes and support Israel, while you keep hemming and hawing without taking a single step? All our colleagues here know that on 9 June 1967, I announced my resignation, and then I was forced to reverse that decision because of the popular pressure for me to stay—in Egypt, in the Arab world, even at the international level. I can carry out this duty until we eliminate the effects of the aggression of 1967. But what I've heard from you and what I've seen on the front is that we have not yet achieved this. I must therefore convey the truth of the matter to the people of Egypt, and to the Arab world, namely, that there is only one real power in the world today, and that is the United States. The people need to accept this, even if they are forced to surrender. But because I will not be the man who surrenders, because my surrender would be unacceptable, I will leave my post to someone capable of this task, such as Zakaria Mohieddin, who will be able to come to an agreement with them.'

Suddenly everyone was talking at once. Tensions in the hall were high. The temperature kept rising until Brezhnev said, 'You're really putting us in a tight spot, you know. Nasser, my dear friend, could you please give us a chance.'

You left the politburo chamber with the Egyptian delegation and waited, your heart pounding. Your fate, the fate of Egypt and the fate of the Arab world were about to be decided in the next few hours, or minutes.

At five o'clock they called you and your aides back into the meeting hall. Brezhnev said through his translator, 'Esteemed Mr President Gamal Abdel Nasser, I would like to inform you that the Soviet leadership and its institutions have unanimously agreed to fulfil all your requests.' That meant they were going to give you the SA-3 missiles and Mikoyan-Gurevich MiG-25 aircraft with Soviet pilots and crew, since it would have taken too long to train Egyptians to fly these planes.

That was how you carried the day.

Intense fighting between Egyptian and Israeli forces on Shadwan Island in the Red Sea.

```
       Israeli paratrooper brigade storms Egyptian
       island in Gulf of Suez under air cover. After
       36 hours of fighting, the enemy withdraws.
                  70 Egyptian casualties.

         Plot uncovered against the South Yemeni
       government. Aden accuses the CIA of conspiring
                with the Muslim Brotherhood.

       Number of executed persons in Iraq reaches 40
          including Rashid Musleh, former interior
               minister, who had helped overthrow
                  Abd al-Karim Qasim in 1963.
          Trials continue in Iraq for 50 others.
```

You'd dealt with power struggles from the very beginning: with Mohamed Naguib, Rashad Mehanna, the Muslim Brotherhood, the communists, Salah and Gamal Salem, Abdel Latif al-Boghdadi, various other ambitious officers, Shams Badran and Abdel Hakim Amer himself. But you always managed to keep the upper hand and dealt with them all, one after the other. Still, you didn't spill blood over it like the Iraqis did. Was there something different about the Egyptian national character?

You picked up Sami al-Jundi's book and flipped through the pages. He was one of the founders of the Iraqi Ba'ath Party. He wrote: 'The ideological origins of violence in the Ba'ath Party stem from the words of its founder, Michel Aflaq, "Successful national struggle requires a powerful hatred towards those who hold opposing values. They must be annihilated so that their ideas too cease to exist."'

Al-Jundi recounted the tragic fate of Staff Brigadier General Abdel Karim Mustafa Nusrat, one of the Ba'ath party leaders who was not on good terms with Salih Mahdi Ammash. A

41

group of Ba'athist soldiers led by the butcher Saddam Hussein broke into Nusrat's bedroom and slaughtered him like a sheep. Then they laid the body out on the mattress, closed the door, and went on their way, while a second group forced Nusrat's servant into his car and drove on to Karbala. There they released him but as soon as he'd walked a few feet they came back and detained him again and called the police, who arrested him on charges of killing Mustafa Nusrat and stealing his car. Under torture, certain agreements were made and his neck was saved in exchange for his confession that he had killed the brigadier general on moral grounds. The Iraqi people were in shock: There was the servant on the television screen, making his confession.

You had always been averse to bloodshed. You refused to support the execution of the king. There were some members of the Revolutionary Command Council who favoured that, but you told them that blood only begets more blood. That time you convinced them, but you did not prevail in the case of the two workers, Mustafa Khamis and Muhammad al-Baqari.

When you executed six Muslim Brotherhood members in 1954 and seven more in 1965, that was because they had resorted to violence and attempted to assassinate you. But you didn't have the same excuse when Shuhdi Atiya was killed under torture in 1960. Before that, six of his comrades were killed in separate incidents of torture. The Egyptian communists had never taken up arms. The same could not be said of you: You'd tried to assassinate Hussein Sirri Amer, a commander in the king's army, just days before the revolution.

The Shuhdi incident happened during the height of your struggle with the communists in Syria and Iraq. You were angry that they'd tried to thwart your dream of a pan-Arab state in which you would hold sole power, and frustrated that they'd insisted on keeping their own positions in the promised union. You turned a blind eye to reports about the crimes that your supporters and associates were committing: Major Abu Nar and his colleague Hamza Bassiouni made blowing up bellies a daily event in the military prison, while Major General Ismail Himmat inflicted sadistic punishments in Abu Zaabal, where torture incidents were followed by indecent games with the younger soldiers. Meanwhile, Hamza Bassiouni enjoyed floggings at the whipping post in Fayoum Prison. There were many different forms of torture, from making prisoners count blades of grass to humiliating dances to the hot skewers used when intelligence officers came to visit. Abdel Hamid al-Sarraj dissolved the body of the general secretary of the Lebanese Communist Party, Farajallah el-Helou, in acid. Still, you weren't against the idea of light torture: it was part of the violent sport that the military played.

Sadat in Banha: We must be prepared for a decisive confrontation with the enemy.

The public meeting was attended by Abdel Mohsen Abou al-Nur, Labib Shuqair, Diaa al-Din Dawoud, members of the Supreme Executive Committee of the Socialist Union, and Socialist Union secretary Shaarawi Gomaa.

Babaker Awadalla, member of the Sudanese National Revolutionary Council: The Arab people believe in Abdel Nasser.

Chicago Tribune correspondent who accompanied Israeli forces during their attack on Shadwan

Island: Despite heavy shelling of the island by
Israeli planes for several hours before their
forces tried to disembark, they encountered fierce
resistance from the Egyptian side. When the
Israelis managed to make land on the north-eastern
side of the island, they repeatedly called over
their loudspeaker for the Egyptian forces to
surrender but were met instead with artillery
shells. All Egyptian positions continued to strike
back until their ammunition ran out. One of those
sites had two soldiers who were captured by the
Israelis. They asked one of the Egyptian soldiers
to go inside a small building near the lighthouse
on the island to convince whoever was there to
surrender. The soldier came back saying he had
found the building empty. An Israeli officer
immediately went with several soldiers to occupy
the building, and they were on the verge of
entering when an Egyptian officer suddenly rained
down fire upon them from his machine gun. The
Israeli officer and some of the soldiers who were
with him were killed. The Egyptian officer was
injured after enemy soldiers overwhelmed him. Two
Egyptian soldiers emerged from another position
pretending to surrender. When the Israeli forces
moved to capture them, a third soldier ambushed
them and fired his machine gun, killing five and
wounding a number of others.

25 January

Egyptian planes launch 5 attacks against the enemy
in a 24-hour period.

Sadat: The valour of our soldiers is a testament
to their devotion to their duty.

Public and military funerals held for the
martyrs of Shadwan.

3 others executed following the
plot in Iraq.

Family mourns the loss of
Naval Lieutenant Colonel Hosni Mohamed Hamad
the martyr and dutiful patriot who led the torpedo
boat that brought reinforcements to forces
stationed on Shadwan Island. As they approached
the island, they were attacked by Israeli planes.
They hid under a smoke screen and pursued a
zig-zag path as they tried to dodge the
airstrikes. Hamad was able to save more than 80
per cent of his men with this tactic before the
boat was hit and he was struck by shrapnel and
martyred. He became a second lieutenant in 1953
and joined the torpedo boats, where he met
Galal Desouky, who was killed in the Tripartite
Aggression in 1956.

Egyptian commando unit destroys enemy radar
station in the Abu Samara area of the Sinai.

50 Israelis killed or injured in Eilat explosion
following a car bomb at the naval port.

Sex-Sex-Sex
at the Global Moqattam Nightclub.
Reserve your seat today.

Third explosion in Beirut this week.

26 January

Half a million people march in Hosni Hamad's
funeral procession in Alexandria.

Cairo was burning. It was a day that would go down in modern Egyptian history, heralding the end of the monarchy. The terrible fire was orchestrated by the king in coordination with the British, along with some of the clandestine groups that the army had been full of before your men came along—or so it seemed. There were Aziz al-Misri's men and Gamal Mansour's, the Military Association for Police and Army Officers, and the Iron Guard—which Yusuf Rashad had organized with Mostafa Kamil Sidqi and Anwar Sadat. Then there were also Abdel Latif al-Boghdadi and Wagih Abaza's men. The Free Officers were in touch with some of these other groups. Perhaps they thought that the fire was going to bring down the monarchy. That was why you permanently ended investigations into the matter. It was a murky and tumultuous time. After this came a period of assassinations and terrorist attacks, and then the military coup and a full-on revolution.

27 January

At dawn, the car took you from the airport in the usual motorcade and set off through the deserted streets. The car came in through the gate to a small courtyard surrounded by the Republican Guard. On the left was a tennis court which had been turned into a cinema, and on the right was the library you'd built where you received the latest books from around the world. Your car stopped in front of the entrance to a small villa: three hundred flowerpots in three rows at different heights and six concrete columns, each with a decorative light that remained lit until three or four in the morning.

You hummed part of a Nagat al-Saghira song, 'Back again, nothing's sweeter'. You were home.

You pulled yourself to your feet and got out of the car, gazing into the back garden. In the far corner there were several chairs, a table and a stone pedestal underneath a big tree. That was where you worked in the summer when the weather was mild enough, the telephone receiver beside you.

The door was decorated with an iron lotus motif, with some Coptic elements in the design. On either side of the door were two German fire extinguishers from 1964. You went into the drawing room. It was twenty feet in each direction with a red-brick and black-marble fireplace. There were eight signed photos in silver frames on the mantel: former Syrian president Shukri al-Quwatli; Sukarno, the president of Indonesia; Nehru, the prime minister of India; Haile Selassie, the emperor of Ethiopia; Tito; Zhou Enlai; and the president of Venezuela. On the right, above the marble slab was a photo of Nkrumah, and on the wall above the fireplace was a big oil painting of two peasant children. The painting was a gift from the Spanish government. On the opposite wall there was a classical painting of a flock of birds. The furniture was arranged geometrically: two large, ornate chairs were placed across from each other in front of the fire-place with a small coffee table in between. This was where you hosted foreign leaders who came to visit. There was a set of gold-leaf Louis XIV-style furniture on the other side of the room—three small tables, a couch and half a dozen chairs upholstered in a heavy embroidered floral brocade. A big crystal chandelier hung from the ceiling. The drawing-room floor was covered in two large eastern-style rugs, with a red-and-blue prayer rug just in front of the fireplace. All of the furniture was government property, though you'd added a number of pieces.

The walls were pale grey with a white ceiling and curtains hung in the windows. The whole house was outfitted with central air-conditioning from Koldair, one of the Egyptian public sector companies.

Two of the windows in the drawing room looked out over a room with a stone-paved floor and a ping pong table, and which had once also contained an electric train set. The two windows were strung with mosquito netting and the ceiling had a small hollow space for electric light fittings.

Your office was on the other side of the hall, across from the drawing room. The far wall was covered in glass bricks. In front of that was a seven-foot-long desk, buried under stacks of reports and newspapers, with a modern high-back leather swivel chair. There was a wooden sideboard with a record player, television and Grundig radio. Guests and servants were not allowed to enter this area, nor family and close friends. You even forbid your daughter's husband Ashraf Marwan from entering when you heard about his antics in London. You walked out of your office into the hall, which led into the dining room. Here the children had inscribed their names on the walls and hung crayon drawings. You could still make out one of these scribbles: Daddy > Khalid.

Next to the dining room there was an antechamber leading to a bathroom with walls covered in pale-blue glazed tiles, and then a reception room that led to the meeting room and then the cinema.

You headed towards the lift. You used to take the wooden stairs at a clip, immersed in conversation with one of the secretaries or children who would come running after you whenever they caught you outside your office. Your wife would always wait for you at the top of the stairs. She was your companion during those tumultuous years, the rock you could always depend upon. Did she not realize how much danger you were in? Or was she just busy looking after the children, and doing embroidery with Heikal's wife? She waited for you with a smile that had begun to betray a flicker of worry. Her smile did wonders for you—it always calmed your nerves. How did she do it?

They opened the door to the lift, which had been installed after your first heart attack. You rode it up to the private family living room with the big Philips television set.

After that you went to your private quarters: another office leading onto your bedroom which faced your wife's bedroom. In the entranceway there was a Westinghouse fridge. On the desk were stacks of paper carefully arranged by Hoda, your eldest daughter, who became your capable new secretary after she graduated from Cairo University. Behind the desk was a bookshelf filled with various books and reference volumes. In one corner of the desk was a stack of journals where you recorded your impressions of events and people. There was a telephone switchboard with eleven buttons next to the desk. If you made a half-turn in your chair and pressed a button, you were connected either with the operator or one of the ten most important men in the government, in their offices or homes. You never knew where you'd catch them. On the other side of the room was a seven-foot couch and a table that held the most powerful radio receiver in Egypt. Above the desk there was a Swiss clock that showed the time anywhere in the world and a portrait of you made of mother-of-pearl.

When you sat down to work, you'd first rummage for a Kent cigarette, which in those days you smoked constantly. You'd glance up at the clock. The newspapers from Beirut arrived via Egypt Air at 7.30 a.m. Your gaze settled on the stacks of papers and files as you hunted for that particular envelope with a red mark on it, which you always kept an eye out for and forbade anyone else from opening.

You opened the envelope and took out the photographs. The photos were of a Lebanese journalist whose daily column you read. He was one of your most devoted supporters, and happened to like men. While he was visiting Cairo your intelligence placed a young man in his path and got a picture of them together. That ensured you had full control over him. Your inteligence did that all the time to exploit various figures, including leading Egyptian actresses and cultural personalities. You let the photos fall from your hand, marvelling at human weakness. You were always proud of your sound mind. Others could rely on you and draw strength from your moral fortitude. You were always particularly pleased when you uncovered their secrets and points of weakness, their heists and infidelities, their exploits with women or with men, their petty ambitions.

7 explosions in Beirut in a single week.

Sadat in meeting with members of professional syndicates' councils: We have rejected the US proposal to resolve the Middle East crisis because they asked Egypt and Israel to agree to ensure free passage through the Gulf of Aqaba and Suez Canal and demanded that the Sinai be demilitarized.

The Fiat 125 is scheduled to begin production next December. Polish factories will provide old car parts for manufacture and assembly by El Nasr

Company in Egypt using locally-manufactured
1500 engines. The first round of production
will include 3,000 cars, gradually increasing to
10,000 by 1975. Egyptian manufacturers will
produce other necessary car parts to eliminate
the need to import.

28 January

Egyptian commando units penetrate 195 km behind
enemy lines east of the canal and strike command
centre with missiles.

Ramses cars (820 LE), now for the
first time sold in instalments
over a 4-year period.

You had travelled to Aswan for a meeting with President Tito
and decided to stay on for a few days after he left. But when your
uncle Khalil Abdel Nasser died the following day, you took the
train from Aswan to Alexandria for the funeral procession.
(You'd previously had him arrested when it came to your attention that he'd had dealings with a French lady. You did not allow
your relatives to take advantage of their connection with you like
that. Once you'd expelled your brother Leithy from the Socialist
Union in Alexandria after various allegations that he had abused
his position for personal benefit.) After that, you returned to
Cairo and found that Israel was absorbed in a bitter assault on
the Egyptian front.

29 January

Nixon announces he has agreed to supply Tel Aviv
with 50 Phantom planes.

Syrian MiG aircraft circle over Haifa without
hostilities from the Israeli forces.

Stop the mini-skirt!
The dean of the College of Fine Arts in Zamalek
receives anonymous threat: If female students are
not barred from wearing mini-skirts, we will burn
down the college.

You didn't particularly care what people wore. You refused to
impose a particular dress code on people because you felt that
it was up to society to figure that out. And you were against the
hijab, which the Muslim Brotherhood wanted to make women
wear. In your famous speech, you denounced their calls to
impose the 'tarha', using the more derogatory popular term for
the headscarf. You had always opposed religious extremism and
the way that it targeted women's work, behaviour and clothing.

31 January

Egyptian infantry company crosses to east bank
of the Suez Canal and destroys a line of enemy
vehicles, killing those inside.

1 February

President Kim Il Sung,
the Great Leader of the Korean revolution.
—*Paid advertisement*

2 February

US representative informs Egypt that Israel
regrets that its airstrikes in the Egyptian
interior have resulted in casualties and advises

Egypt to immediately accept a ceasefire or
airstrikes will continue to escalate.

The Islamic world and legal field grieve the
loss of Dr Mohamed Abdullah Elaraby,
God rest his soul.
The deceased is the father of Dr Nabil Elaraby,
first secretary of the Ministry of Foreign
Affairs, and a relative of Mrs Anwar Sadat
and of Mr Mahmoud Abu Wafia,
Sadat's brother-in-law.

3 February

Abdel Nasser at the Inter-Parliamentary
Conference: The US is responsible for what is
happening now and what is about to happen.

Egyptian commandos cross Suez Canal near al-Tor
and strike the enemy's military installations with
missiles.

Egyptian Cabinet to allow emigration for
certain professions if local labour needs have
already been met.

Umm Kulthum
to sing two new songs in her monthly concert
to be held the day after tomorrow and broadcast
from the Qasr El Nil Theatre.

How you used to look forward to those nights! You'd go up to
your bedroom bringing with you the foreign newspapers and
magazines. Your bed was to the left of the door, with a large
stack of meticulously organized papers beside it. There was a

television and a small radio to the left of the bed, and across from the door was a built-in wardrobe closet which had a mirror in the middle above a chiffonier. You'd sit for a moment in the rocking chair and then take off your work clothes and turn on the radio next to the bed and spend the next hour or two reading. You loved the photos in French magazines, the advertisements in *LIFE* and *TIME* and cartoon strips. But you broke this routine on the first Thursday of each month when Umm Kulthum sang. You had begun listening to her songs when you fell for your first love, Souad, whose features were now hard for you to recall. That was all before the catastrophe of 1967. Now you just lay back in bed holding the telephone receiver to your ear, waiting for news to come in.

5 February

Abdel Nasser and Hussein meet today
in preparation for the Conference of
Frontline Countries.

Soviet newspaper *Izvestia*:
Israel prepares for total war.

Exodus of doctors: An increasing number of
doctors affiliated with the Ministry of Health are
emigrating to the US, Canada, Australia
and Brazil—500 in the last year.

6 February

Egyptian frogmen explode two Israeli vessels
carrying tanks and soldiers in the Port of Eilat.

Lieutenant General Haim Bar-Lev, IDF chief of
general staff, admits that the operation was well
executed and a complete success.

Egyptian fighter-bombers strike enemy troops in
al-Shatt and Oyun Musa; Enemy launches
counter-strikes in civilian areas in Asyut,
Hurghada and Safaga.

Kosygin warns: The crisis is no longer confined
to the Middle East. It has become a threat to
global peace.

Soviet Union provides Arab forces with all
necessary means to repel the enemy.

In stores now:
Third edition of the records 'The Roving Bird'
and 'The Washtub Told Me'.

Metro Cinema presents:
Rock Hudson on a dangerous mission
as the world's two greatest powers come
head-to-head.

Reports from Washington indicate that Nixon has
agreed to provide Israel with 105 planes.

7 February

President Abdel Nasser welcomes Sudanese President
Major General Jaafar Nimeiry and Syrian President
Dr Nureddin al-Atassi upon their arrival at the
Cairo airport, and accompanies them to
al-Qubba Palace. They were later joined by King
Hussein and Lieutenant General Salih Mahdi Ammash,
the head of the Iraqi delegation.

10 February

Major air combat between 42 Egyptian and
Israeli aircraft.

2 enemy planes downed, including one over
Lake Manzala.

The battle lasted for an hour and all our planes
returned safely. The clashes began following a
successful airstrike by our fighter planes at
4.30 p.m. on enemy positions on the east bank of
the Suez Canal. As they returned to their bases
after the mission, they were followed by about
12 enemy Mirage planes. The Egyptian side had air
cover waiting, which clashed with the enemy planes
that had tried to follow our aircraft. The enemy
was forced to bring in reinforcements and soon
there were 22 Israeli planes against the
20 Egyptian MiG-21 planes.
The battle lasted for a full hour.

Surprise decision by Jordanian Cabinet to prohibit
bearing arms, publishing magazines or pamphlets or
holding meetings without permission from the
authorities, excepting resistance factions aligned
with the Jordanian government.

President Abdel Nasser receives Yasser Arafat
before the PLO chairman travels to Moscow.

Libyan military tribunal held for 30 suspects
accused of 'plotting to overthrow the
revolutionary government'. Suspects include former
minister of the interior and minister of defence.

12 February

Egyptian infantry company crosses the canal
and destroys enemy targets in the early morning.
At noon our fighter planes struck enemy positions
in El Balah and Deversoir. In the evening our
anti-aircraft defences brought down an Israeli
plane east of Port Fuad.

Israeli Phantoms strike Abu Zaabal rebar
factory with missiles and napalm. The factory cost
5 million LE and employs 2,000 workers supporting
2,600 families. 80 people were killed and 60
wounded in the attack.

US angered by Egyptian military operations
against Israel.

8 Palestinians killed in clashes between
Palestinian resistance forces and Jordanian
authorities.

Despite the recent ban, Palestinian fedayeen
continue to roam the streets of the Jordanian
capital with their weapons. They have built
barricades and trenches around their offices and
gathering points. Since telephone service has been
cut off to most of these locations, the fedayeen
leaders rely on radios to communicate.

Faten Hamama visits Cairo:
After five years abroad, the First Lady of Arabic
Cinema returns to Egypt for a two-week visit by
invitation of the General Cinema Foundation.

13 February

Tito: The time has come to take serious action against Israel.

Pravda:
Egyptian armed forces have entered a new stage of active defence against Israel.

Egyptian fighter-bombers strike enemy targets in the canal twice.

Abdel Nasser and Gaddafi hold a two-hour meeting starting at 8.15 p.m. The meeting with President Abdel Nasser was attended by Hussein al-Shafei, Abdel Mohsen Abou al-Nur, Dr Labib Shuqair, members of the Supreme Executive Committee of the Socialist Union and Minister Fathi al-Dib.

Bloody clashes in Amman during talks between King Hussein and members of the 10 resistance organizations.
19 resistance fighters and government Desert Forces killed.

Baligh Hamdi composes works for his brother Mursi Saad al-Din: Baligh has prepared four songs that will be performed by Shadia in a film written by Mursi Saad al-Din, and which also stars Shadia's husband, Salah Zulfikar. The screenplay was written by Youssef Francis and the dialogue by Abdel Rahman el-Abnudi. Baligh had also finished 22 compositions of short songs for the film *Lights of the City* which will star Shadia along with Ahmed Mazhar, Abdel Moneim Ibrahim, Adel Imam, Hassan Mustafa and 'Triple Fun'.

Chickens for Eid:
For Eid al-Adha, subsidized stores in Cairo
and Alexandria will sell fine Danish chickens for
the same price as local chickens, butchered with a
sharp knife as per Islamic procedure.

You went to a Cabinet meeting which you headed. You picked up a bag from beside you and placed it on the table, where you opened it and took out several loaves of bread. You turned to Dr Kamal Ramzi Stino, minister of supply, and rebuked him, 'Would you eat this bread, Dr Kamal?'

'No, sir, I would not,' he answered.

You said, 'Well, that's what's coming out of your bakeries these days. I had these brought from all over Cairo. If you wouldn't eat this yourself, how can you accept that this is what people are given to eat? The average citizen buys ten pieces of bread every day. Is this bread edible? Well, Dr Kamal? You have forty-eight hours to fix this situation.'

14 February

King Hussein: The internal procedures that led to
this crisis with the resistance groups did not
target them in any way.

16 February

400 US planes bomb Laos.

17 February

Sirens sound this afternoon in Cairo after enemy
planes breach Egyptian airspace.

19 February

192 million LE worth of goods imported into Egypt
within the past 6 months.

20 February

Egyptian planes surprise enemy twice and strike
Israeli encampments in the Bitter Lakes
and al-Qantara.

Jordanian army lays siege to Amman
and Palestinian resistance declares another state
of emergency.

21 February

Soviet Union rejects US ceasefire proposal because
it would not include a full withdrawal of Israeli
forces.

Second Israeli plane downed in a 24-hour period.

Swiss plane explodes after taking off from
Zurich Airport en route to Tel Aviv. All 47
passengers killed.

25 February

Jordanian talks with the resistance begin.

Jordanian Interior Minister Rasoul al-Kilani
resigns.

Kuwait condemns US policy in the Middle East.

New cars imported without currency conversion.

New issue of *al-Hilal* magazine:
100th anniversary of Lenin's birth.

Read all about:
Yusuf al-Sibai — Gamal Kamel — Hassan Fuad —
Kamal al-Mallakh — Amina al-Said — Ahmed al-Hadary
— Hussein Bicar — Salah Taher — Mostafa Darwish —
Abd al-Rahman Sidqi — Saleh Gawdat — Kamal al-Najmi
— Salah Hafez — Diaa Baybars — Tharwat Abaza —
Louis Awad — Ibrahim al-Wardani — Youssef Francis
— Latifa Saleh — Naguib Mahfouz — Helmi el-Touni —
Anis Mansour — Nadia Lutfi — Youssef Gohar.

26 February

Air battle on the northern coast of the delta
between 16 Egyptian and Israeli planes;
3 Israeli Phantom and Mirage planes downed.

28 February

Executions continue in Iraq.

The number of illegitimate children born to US
soldiers in South Vietnam has reached 20,000.
Vietnamese minister states that this phenomenon
is a blessing since introducing new blood into
society leads to stronger offspring.

3 March

Bold attack by the resistance in Gaza.

West German government announces it is willing to
pay new reparations to 180,000 Jews.

New spring and summer styles from
El Nasr Company for Spinning, Weaving
and Knitting: al-Shourbagy mini-bikini
modelled by Ragaa al-Geddawy.

5 March

Dayan admits to using napalm in airstrikes.

March was an eventful month for you. In March 1954, you dealt with your first major crisis and almost lost everything—yet managed to capably steer a path forward.

You had carefully studied the character of each of your colleagues in the founding committee of the Free Officers, which later became the Revolutionary Command Council. They were a motley crew: the two brothers, Salah and Gamal Salem, who were a little peculiar, and Abdel Moneim Amin—he and his wife were closely connected to the US embassy. Then there was Abdel Moneim Raouf, a Muslim Brotherhood member; Khaled Mohieddin, who was part of the Democratic Movement for National Liberation (Haditu), a communist organization; and Abdel Latif al-Boghdadi, a formidable man who rarely said anything.

Just twenty days after the revolution of 1952, the workers of Kafr el-Dawwar went on strike for the right to form an independent union free from their bosses' control. They demanded wages commensurate with the rising cost of living, as Mostafa el-Nahas' government had promised, the pay rises and full rations that the Wafd government was supposed to deliver, and an end to arbitrary dismissals. After the workers demonstrated for the removal of the factory and company managers, the police commissioner showed up and ordered the doors of the factory shut and then fired two shots from his pistol and arrested some of the workers.

The workers announced that two of their comrades had been killed and called for an ambulance, and when none appeared, they began throwing bricks. The next afternoon two marches were organized by the workers and their families, who set off with sticks and tree branches towards the factory to free the detained workers. Before they crossed the Kilometre 5 Bridge they ran into army forces led by Major Mohammed Nagi. The army arrested the young worker Mustafa Khamis who had been leading the protest. The army fired on them, killing five and wounding twenty-two. During this incident one of the company buildings caught fire.

The armed forces command issued a statement that evening, signed by Major General Mohamed Naguib, which described the workers as 'traitors with ulterior motives, who aimed to hinder the army's efforts to enact social reform'. It went on to say that the army had been compelled to intervene and that Prime Minister Aly Maher Pasha had agreed to form a high military tribunal to prosecute those responsible.

The Muslim Brotherhood was quick to condemn the Kafr el-Dawwar workers' strikes, drawing on the legal opinions of Sayyid Qutb. Members of Haditu tried to placate the workers and prevent a clash with the new government, believing as they did in its nationalism—and were consequently accused of treachery by the other communist groups in Egypt and beyond.

The military tribunal was convened in the middle of the factory the next day. It was led by Colonel Abdel Moneim Amin, a member of the Revolutionary Command Council. Musa Sabry, an *Akhbar el-Yom* journalist, volunteered to defend Mustafa Khamis in this farce. The ruling—execution by hanging—was issued two days later. It was announced in the company yard, where the military had assembled thousands of workers, who stood in terror.

Then a second trial began: twenty-six workers before the same tribunal. As the military public prosecutor put it, he had seen 'heads ripe for plucking', as in days of yore. The first defendant, Muhammad al-Baqari, was sentenced to death by hanging, while the rest of the defendants got hard labour.

As the Revolutionary Command Council discussed the sentences before ratifying them, Major Abdel Halim Abdel Mutaal, a Free Officer, accused Hafez Afifi Pasha, the chief of King Farouk's royal cabinet and one of the main shareholders in the Misr Fine Spinning and Weaving Company, of plotting the killings and sabotaging the workers' peaceful demonstrations.

However, the majority still decided to approve the sentences. You warned them again that blood only begets more blood. You expressed your opposition to the executions, though you also privately felt that they were a useful deterrent against that huge and mysterious force—the workers—which the communists were trying to take control of.

There was heated debate—and new hope—among the Revolutionary Command Council and the Free Officers after the king was deposed. Would parliamentary life return and the country's affairs be placed in the hands of the Wafd government? Would the officers go back to their barracks or would they stay in power? In the latter case, who was going to be in charge? You sat in that critical meeting and knew what they were going to say. You told them that you personally felt it would be better to hand over control to the political parties and have the officers go back to their barracks, rather than set up a dictatorship. As you expected, most of the men were of the opposing view and the majority prevailed. You decided together to abolish political parties and take executive and legislative power for yourselves, until a new constitution was established three years later.

Then in 1954 a democratic tide swept through the country, led by Khaled Mohieddin and Mohamed Naguib, who was lured on by dreams of taking power for himself. You agreed that the army would go back to the barracks. At the same time, you were secretly working with Taima, al-Tahawi and Bultiya to organize anti-democratic protests. This culminated in the tram workers' strike which you arranged just by paying the head of the union 4,000 LE. He was unaffectionately known as 'cuckoo' after that. You were also behind the bombings at Cairo University and Maison Groppi. In the end, it all worked out in your favour: You became president while Khaled Mohieddin was removed from the Revolutionary Command Council and then sent abroad for a while. Meanwhile, Mohamed Naguib was held under house arrest in a villa belonging to Zeinab al-Wakil, who was el-Nahas' wife. Naguib was scrubbed out of the history books once and for all. Now the history of the Republic of Egypt could begin with you, and you alone.

6 March

US ambassador informs Lebanese President Charles Helou that even if Israel were to follow through on its threat to retaliate against Lebanon following the resistance operations, this would be limited in scope—it would not carry out a large-scale military operation.

Israeli airstrikes target Jordan.

Al-Hobb al-Kabir:
Farid al-Atrash's most ambitious musical comedy
to date.

7 March

Air battles at the front; enemy loses 3 planes.

Israeli forces attack village on Lebanese border.

Week of the female fedayeen:
Fatima Bernawi, who was sentenced to life
imprisonment after being arrested during the
bombing incident at the cinema in Jerusalem;
Shadia Abu Ghazaleh, who carried out several
military operations and died accidentally detonating
a bomb she was making; Rashida Abdel Rahim, who
set off a bomb in the main market in Jerusalem;
Maryam Shakhshir of Nablus, who was accused of
detonating a bomb at the Hebrew
University and whose whereabouts are still
unknown; Nabila al-Wazir, a student from Gaza
who was accused of forming a network of female
students to resist the occupation and was
sentenced to life imprisonment; and Samia Ali
from the city of al-Bireh, who is currently held
at the Moscovia Detention Centre.

No matter how late
They'll come, come soon,
From the road to Ramallah, from Jabal al-Zeitoun
They'll come, come soon.
—Nizar Qabbani

You went out alone for one of your spontaneous excursions. You'd take a regular car, a smaller one, on occasions like Sham al-Naseem, during Ramadan, or at the beginning of the new school year. While you were out, you'd observe people's behaviour, examine their clothing styles and facial expressions and see how the people were getting along with the police. Maybe you were inspired by the two Umars—Umar ibn al-Khattab and Umar ibn Abd al-Aziz—who used to make their rounds by night to see how their subjects were doing. You noticed this year that all the girls were wearing bright-coloured dresses, and wondered if that meant anything. Was morale up since last year?

9 March

First anniversary of the passing of
Abdel Moneim Riad
who was martyred right on the canal,
150 metres away from the enemy.

Another blow. You'd had such confidence in him as chief of staff of the armed forces, as he worked with Fawzi, the minister of war, to rebuild fighting capabilities.

11 March

Resistance bombs Israeli post office and
employment office in Gaza.

12 March

President Ahmed Hassan al-Bakr delivers Iraqi
Revolutionary Command Council statement regarding
a peaceful and democratic solution to the Kurdish
question. He stated that an agreement had been
reached that recognized the Kurdish right to a
nation, enabled Kurds to govern Kurdish regions,
promised the appointment of a Kurdish
vice president for Iraq, recognized their
linguistic and cultural rights
and made Newroz a national holiday.

13 March

Egyptian Air Defence Forces repel Israeli
airstrikes on Sursuq village near Mansoura.

16 March

Waves of Israeli airstrikes on the northern
section of the canal between Port Said and
Ismailia continue for 5 hours.
Egyptian Air Defence brings down
one Skyhawk.

17 March

Ezer Weizman, hours before travelling to the US:
With regard to the peace initiatives that some
have proposed, Theodor Herzl's is the only one
I've heard of that might lead to peace. (This

would mean establishing a state from the Euphrates
to the Nile which would include half
of Iraq, Syria, Lebanon, Jordan, the Sinai,
the Delta, Cairo and the Egyptian desert
down to Qena.)

18 March

Egyptian aircraft fight back 3 Israeli airstrikes
on Egyptian positions.

20 March

Soviet SA-3 missiles arrive in Egypt
along with their technical crews.
The sophisticated missile defence is used
against low-altitude planes.

21 March

Nixon: The US will take immediate action to ensure
Israel's security if it appears that Soviet
weapons shipments to Egypt have changed the
balance of military power in the Middle East.

15,000 Arabs behind bars in Israel.

Minister of Culture Tharwat Okasha convenes the
board of the theatre association and forms
committees led by Abdel Aziz al-Ahwani, Louis
Awad, Rushdi Saleh and Lotfy El Kholy.

Egyptian commandos destroy oil rig that Israel
had intended to use in the Gulf of Suez.
The bold operation took place in the port of
Abidjan, the capital of the Republic of the Ivory
Coast, in West Africa.

23 March

Demonstrators in Beirut protest attacks on resistance forces in Bint Jbeil in southern Lebanon during clashes between the resistance and Lebanese army patrol, following a resistance operation against Israeli positions in the Upper Galilee.

Cairo Cinema:
The Detective starring Jacqueline Bisset (Adults only).

Faisal launches Islamic Conference of Foreign Ministers to follow up on the resolutions made at the Rabat conference regarding liberating Jerusalem and restoring the legitimate rights of the Palestinian people.

New play starring Farid Shawqi:
The Marsh Snipes.

President Abdel Nasser welcomes Muhammad Ali Haitham, member of the Yemeni Presidential Council and prime minister of the People's Republic of South Yemen.

Our fighters repel enemy planes during airstrikes on Balṭim and al-Qantara.

24 March

Violent clashes between Palestinian resistance and Kataeb militias in Lebanon.

25 March

Rogers' statements openly hostile to Arabs.

Ahmed Sadek, chief of the general staff of the
Egyptian Armed Forces, promoted to rank of
lieutenant general.

3 killed and 14 wounded in hostilities by
unidentified aggressor against the resistance
fighters on the outskirts of Beirut. Palestinian
Liberation Army commander says that the US embassy
has spent a million dollars on incitement against
the resistance.

Your mind wandered, thinking about how things were going. Your development plan had been successful, resulting in 6.5 per cent growth between 1957 and 1967 without reliance on foreign aid. But although the socioeconomic landscape had changed, you realized that the system you'd created was really in crisis. Corruption was rampant and people were fed up with the restrictions on their liberties as a result of the ongoing conflict with the colonizers and reactionary powers, and the tight grip the intelligence agencies kept on society. If one of your colleagues in the Revolutionary Council wanted to be alone with his wife, he'd go out without giving anyone notice and rent a room in a hotel. People were also frustrated about the war in Yemen.

You realized that a new class had emerged, which was initially composed of former army officers, including some of the Free Officers, whom you had removed from the army and given civilian positions. At first some had taken up positions with the Poultry Company, in the Abd el-Aziz Street branch of the Omar Effendi department store or at the front desk of the Hilton. But they quickly became businessmen and most of them got involved with the oil sheikhs' agents and reactionary groups.

The officers' relatives began to fill company boards of directors, the Suez Canal Authority, the army and the judiciary.

Some of your men, especially Zakaria Mohieddin and Abdel Moneim al-Kaissouni, had begun to call for downsizing—which was also the IMF and World Bank's advice. You'd heard Zakaria say that the fellahin had spent all their lives wearing one galabiyya and now they had two—so it wouldn't be a problem to go back to a single galabiyya for a while if that was what development required. Plus the price of a kilo of milk had gone up from 6 to 8 piasters. And there were tales of the refrigerators and air conditioning units and television sets that Field Marshal Amer's associates got from Yemen to sell on the black market, and of the trafficking in licenses for Nasr cars. There was also the saga of Amer's marriage to an actress he was introduced to by the head of intelligence, Salah Nasr, not to mention the tales of Salah's corruption.

Several weeks before the military defeat, you had realized that this was no longer about the individuals involved—it was a crisis for the whole regime. As you put it: The regime as it currently stands leaves the fate of the country to a single man but having only one party at this time, under these conditions, has become a dangerous game. This could lead to a passive populace who'd leave the most important decisions to bureaucrats or technocrats. You said: We must therefore expand the process of reorganizing the opposition forces so that they have outlets through which to express their ideas to the people and to monitor the behaviour of the state.

But the opposition you were talking about was a calculated opposition which would remain under your control.

27 March

Air battle in the Gulf of Suez between 40 Israeli
and Egyptian planes; 3 Israeli planes sustain
damage.

28 March

Evacuation of the last British soldier from Libyan
territory and British bases liquidated.

Another ordeal. Two years ago—for the first time since 1954—
there had been protests against you. That was after the trial of
the Air Force commanders over their responsibility for the defeat
of 1967. People were expecting executions and were taken aback
by the lenient sentences. The workers in the war factories that
you had built in Helwan went out to protest and the Socialist
Union men couldn't rein them in. The person in charge of the
local organizing was Abdel Latif Bultiya, who had been one of
the champions of the now-defunct Liberation Rally.

They clashed with the police and shots were fired. Two people were killed and nine wounded. The students in the faculty
of engineering at Cairo University, where your son Khalid studied, staged a sit-in calling for freedom of opinion, freedom of
the press and the dissolution of the Socialist Union. They
demanded that spies and informants be kept out of universities
and chanted: 'Down with the intelligence state!', 'Down with the
military state!', 'Down with Heikal's lies!', 'Hey Gamal, we are
the people, so kick out the traitors!' and 'Hey Shaarawi, you
coward, where are the workers from Helwan?' The remnants of
the right wing seized the opportunity. The Judges' Club, which
had been taken over by a group led by Wafdist judge Mumtaz

Nassar, issued a statement criticizing the regime and calling for the independence of the judiciary and for democracy. That was when you lost your patience and said, 'Well, if we can't lead, then we will rule.' You decided to institute some major changes in personnel and institutions, issued the 30 March Statement and put together a new Cabinet with fresh faces under your own leadership. For a time, it seemed that things were headed in a new direction but you can't teach an old dog new tricks, as they say.

Among the new ministers was Dr Hilmi Murad, who was Ahmed Hussain's brother-in-law and one of the old socialists. He had been president of Aim Shams University and was an active member of the Vanguard Organization. He'd taken an excellent stance during the student protests and would be able to resolve the situation democratically without security interventions. You appointed him as minister of education, which was a ministry that you had often overlooked and left to reactionaries like El-Sayed Youssef, your sister-in-law's husband, and Kamal el-Din Hussein. Murad had also been involved in implementing the 30 March Statement and had written you two letters. The first was on the conflict that had flared up between Minister of Justice Abu Nusair and the Judges' Club and culminated in what became known as the Massacre of the Judges. He had advised you to settle the matter before it got out of hand. The second letter objected to the censoring of an interview he'd given with the *Rose al-Yusuf* magazine about the 30 March Statement. In a Cabinet meeting, you expressed your displeasure about the two letters and left in a huff after declaring that Hilmi Murad was impossible to work with. After that Murad stopped going to his office in the ministry and on 10 July 1969 was relieved of his position.

The truth was plain and clear. You couldn't tolerate any opposition, even from those closest to you. In 1962, you held a National Congress of Popular Forces, which was one of your strategies for dealing with crises—in this case the split with Syria. Anwar Salama, who was backed by the regime and had been made president of the Egyptian Trade Union Federation, stood up to speak on behalf of the Federation in order to make certain demands. You were furious—no one could force you to give what you gave the working class. You did not take orders!

31 March

250,000 people march in Khartoum on Sunday to mourn the victims of civil strife provoked by some of the Ansar (followers of al-Mahdi's family and the National Umma Party), who were armed with swords and spears. National Socialist Front blames foreign interference.

70 members selected for the general committee for the citizens' war committees. Minister of Social Affairs Hafez Badawi to lead committee. Members to include Muhammad Abd al-Salam al-Zayyat, secretary-general of the National Assembly and member of the Socialist Union's Central Committee; Fathy Ghanem, chairman of the Dar al-Tahrir board of directors; Abdel Latif Bultiya, head of the Egyptian Trade Union Federation; Fuad Mursi al-Haddad, a member of the National Assembly and leader of one of the dissolved communist organizations; Kamal Hennawy;

Abou Seif Youssef, a leader from the same
communist group; Ahmed Baha al-Din, head of Dar
al-Hilal publishing house; Ahmed Fuad, head of
Banque Misr; and Mamdouh Salem,
the governor of Asyut.

1 April

Civil strife put down in Sudan despite popular
support for revolution. 180 casualties on Aba
Island.

You sent Sadat, who was joined by Air Force officer Hosni
Mubarak, to help Nimeiry deal with the Mahdist rebellion on
Aba Island. Sadat wanted the Egyptian planes already deployed
there to hit them hard with airstrikes but you refused. The
leader of the rebellion, al-Hadi al-Mahdi, was assassinated by
explosives hidden in a basket of mangoes. There were some
indications that Hosni Mubarak might have been the one who
had sent the basket.

State of emergency in the Libyan army.

12 martyred and 35 injured in Israeli airstrike
on the northern Egyptian delta.

UN Secretary General U Thant meets with
representatives of 13 Bahraini organizations to
discuss the future of the emirate after British
forces withdraw at the end of this year.

More than 85 doctors not granted permission to
emigrate this year after 400 doctors left the
Ministry of Health last year to the US, Canada,
Australia and Brazil.

3 April

Israel strikes Syrian positions; land and air battles continue all day.

Mystery surrounds Royal Air Maroc plane crash in Casablanca; 61 people dead.

Palestinian resistance organizations meet to work towards unity.

'The Days Went By'
Umm Kulthum's full performance on
33 rpm record, 3 LE.

Belmont King Size
the Arabs' favourite cigarette.

Ferro China Romani
Quality quinine tonic.

4 April

Air battle in the middle of the delta between 30 Egyptian and Israeli planes.

Faysal al-Shaabi, former prime minister of South Yemen, is killed attempting to escape from the detention camp where he was held.

Former Sudanese Prime Minister Sadiq al-Mahdi seeks refuge in Cairo.

5 April

20-inch Telemisr TV available for the first time in the UAR, 125 LE.

6 April

Lieutenant General Hafez al-Assad, the Syrian
minister of defence, visits the Syrian front.

Soutelphan presents Abdel Halim Hafez and
Nadia Lutfi in *Dad's Up the Tree*.

7 April

Egyptian unit penetrates 60 km past enemy lines
and strikes assembled forces with missiles.

Abdel Khaliq Mahjub, secretary general of the
disbanded Sudanese Communist Party, arrives in
Cairo after being expelled by the Sudanese
government; Egyptian government agrees to let
Mahjub stay.

You put him under your surveillance with help from your
trusted associate Ahmed Hamroush. He was a Free Officer who
had been a member of Haditu. He was still in contact with them
and became your eyes in Haditu and your channel of communication with the group.

75 years ago in *al-Ahram*:
The Lady from Suez performs at the mawlid of
Ahmad al-Badawi: The famous singer is coming to
Tanta with her accompanists to perform at the
lesser mawlid of Ahmad al-Badawi at Paolo's famed
coffeehouse and guesthouse, an establishment known
for its excellent location, quality drinks,
delicious fare, cleanliness, professional service
and abundance of revelry and merriment. Mr Paolo
invites lovers of music and leisure to grace the

coffeehouse and guesthouse with their company for
what promises to be a pleasant evening.

8 April

Israeli massacre at the Bahr al-Baqar School:
Five Israeli Phantom planes carried out an
airstrike on a primary school in al-Husseiniya
in Sharqia governorate this morning
and dropped 5 bombs weighing 1,000 pounds
and 2 missiles, which resulted in the complete
destruction of the school. 30 children were killed
and 50 more injured.

Sudanese Minister of the Economy Ahmed Sulaiman,
one of the leaders of the Sudanese Communist
Party loyal to Jaafar Nimeiry, announces that
Major General Nimeiry, head of the Revolutionary
Council, will soon issue decisions to liberate the
economy from foreign control.

King of Jordan awards Abdel Halim Hafez the Order
of Independence after he sang in the wedding of
the king's sister, Princess Basma.

Third anniversary of the passing of
the martyr and hero
Lieutenant Adel Ibrahim Qansuh.

School in Agouza expels a thanawiyya amma student
who insisted on wearing a mini-skirt.

9 April

Flights of Israeli Phantom planes strike Egyptian
positions in the central section of the canal and
injure 4 soldiers.

10 April

Sudan expels US commercial attaché.

Al-Tali'a magazine, published by al-Ahram, has invited two top Soviet thinkers to give lectures about Lenin's position on national liberation and on Zionism and Judaism.

12 April

Resistance forces storm Israeli industrial area near Sedom and attack potash factories.

13 April

878 Israelis killed or injured during past year on the canal front alone.

Postage stamp of Lenin to be issued in Cairo on 21 April to mark the centennial of his birth.

Central Committee of the Arab Socialist Union celebrates the occasion with Vice President Anwar Sadat, the Soviet ambassador, Dr Mahmoud Fawzi, Dr Labib Shuqair and Shaarawi Gomaa, minister of the interior and secretary general of the Socialist Union.

You were walking that fine line again. You had to keep the Soviets happy—they were obsessed with how things looked. At the same time, you wanted to provoke the right wing's ire against the leftists who were gaining ground and thereby clear out some of the leftists without losing your standing with the Soviets. You forced them to stomach your success in liquidating the communist movement in Egypt—something many before you had failed to achieve.

Your most brutal campaign against the communists was in 1959, when you used all the tools at your disposal. You lied and accused them of working as Russian or Bulgarian agents, although you were aware from personal experience that they had their own take on things and even disagreed with the Soviets sometimes. There was no evidence at all of financial ties or anything like that. It was particularly shrewd that you accused them before the masses of trying to set up a 'dictatorship of the *proletariat*', using that foreign expression instead of 'the working class'. In early 1959 you threw hundreds of them in prison (even though the communists in Haditu had supported you through thick and thin). You brought their leaders before military tribunals, with Major General Hilal Abdullah Hilal as judge. He'd been one of the first to flee in the Sinai in 1967 as the Israeli tanks approached. In the prisons and detention centres, you gave them a taste of all kinds of brutal military sport!

Shuhdi Atiya, a prominent communist and the political leader of Haditu, was killed under torture in 1960, triggering an international outcry that put an end to those sprees. Then you moved into the second, more difficult stage, which lasted until 1964: infiltrating and co-opting the communists by relaxing some of the prison rules (allowing books and newspapers to be smuggled in, and letting them listen to Umm Kulthum), waving around the possibility that they'd be released if they swore to stay out of politics, and eventually hinting at a general amnesty for all prisoners. But the main reason your plan succeeded was your own ideological development from your constant reading, as you worked out how you might achieve your dream of social justice and prosperity for the Egyptian people. Sometimes you went beyond their wildest dreams: nationalizing major companies, getting workers into the boards of directors, lowering rents, banning arbitrary dismissals of workers —not to mention your resolutely anti-colonial stance and resistance to reactionary schemes. Because of this, some communists (mainly in Haditu) saw you as a newcomer to the growing socialist camp.

You had a long history with the communists of Haditu.

Your young colleague Khaled Mohieddin had been a member of Haditu before the revolution. As you tried to get a grasp of the various political organizations, you let him organize a meeting for you with the judge Ahmed Fuad, who was one of the leaders of Haditu. You met together at Khaled's house and liked what he had to say, so after that you invited the officers in Haditu to join the Free Officers, provided that they joined on an individual basis and not as part of their organization. They agreed. You went with Khaled to visit Ahmed Fuad at his home, where you found another man was already there, whom Ahmed Fuad introduced to you as his friend Badr. The way Badr talked politics impressed you. When you left the house with Khaled, you asked him about this mysterious Badr, well-spoken and open-minded, and he said he was the secretary general of Haditu. You asked, 'So what does he do for work?' Khaled answered, 'He's the secretary general.' You asked again, sharply, 'I mean, what was he doing before he became secretary general?' 'He was a mechanic,' Khaled said. You cried out, 'You mean the members of this party take orders from a mechanic?'

That really stuck with you, especially once you learnt that he'd been a mechanic in the Air Force. A mechanic! You kept coming back to that—disapprovingly, sometimes with open scorn. Even after the coup, when tensions heated up during Revolutionary Command Council meetings, you once said, gesturing to Khaled, 'They've got a mechanic in charge.' That was why you were averse to that group in particular.

Later, in 1964, when you felt that your policy of carrots and sticks had almost run its course and that most communists were ready to accept your leadership and consider working with the Socialist Union, you moved instead into a new phrase of liquidating them.

You had formed the (secret) Vanguard Organization in mid-1963 with an ideological premise that wasn't so different from theirs. You made sure that prisoners heard about this new organization and knew they'd be welcome to join. Some communists who hadn't been imprisoned, or the old guard who had given up active work, did in fact join, on the condition they cut all previous ties. The doors of the Socialist Union—both its official side, and its secret organizations—were open to communists as long as they left the party.

Khrushchev was set to visit Egypt for the ceremony celebrating the diversion of the Nile during the construction of the Aswan High Dam. He made clear that it would cause embarrassment back home if he were to visit a country with prisons full of communists. Egypt was already suffocating under police pressure and needed a valve. You decided the time had come to release those worn down by the walls of prison and all that was happening outside.

They were released in waves. You seemed to have some reservations or else there was some other entity that didn't want the prisoners released. There was a bloody incident at al-Wahat Prison in which one of the communist prisoners was killed. Several attempts were made to put off or stall their release. The last group was let go into the streets the night before Khrushchev came, instead of through the prison's usual discharge procedures, which took several days.

During this time, you continued to make clear that you welcomed the unity of all socialist forces and would not tolerate any underground political activity, which you would once again be compelled to put down.

In December 1964, the General Secretariat of the Socialist Union was formed. It included Khaled Mohieddin and a number of leftist figures. Khaled was the press secretary and Ibrahim Saad Eddin was secretary of the Socialist Institute. There was a blanket amnesty issued for all communist cases and accessory penalties were dropped. You formed a special committee led by Zakaria Mohieddin's chief of staff to find suitable positions for the communists who had been let out, but the committee dragged its feet in dealing with those newly-released workers.

The idea of merging Haditu and the Vanguard Organization was brought up in meetings that you held with Ahmed Hamroush and leaders like Kamal Abdel Halim, a political official for Haditu. Abdel Halim had suffered some kind of nervous breakdown because of the torture he was subjected to in the military prison in 1953. In the end Haditu agreed to join the Vanguard Organization. A full chart of all the members of Haditu was prepared, with plans to put them with various members of the Vanguard Organization. Ahmed Fuad brought you the chart and you were upset about how rushed the whole thing was, so you quickly backtracked and had them join as individuals rather than merging the two organizations.

Haditu ultimately pulled out, licking their wounds. They were under various kinds of pressure (including death threats in one case) and were tossing around this idea of dissolving the organization and joining the Socialist Union one by one. After a decisive meeting they were still on the fence when Kamal Abdel Halim suggested that the organization be vested in him. After they agreed, Haditu was officially dissolved. Kamal Abdel Halim rushed to the post office in Tahrir Square to send a telegram congratulating you on this decision.

The same drama played out with the other party involved in communist activity alongside Haditu. But they were also different: First they accused you of being a military fascist and then only a capitalist, until they finally saw the light. This party was also unusual because some of the leaders were the scions of notables and feudalists who had rebelled against their families. Heikal was your go-between here: He liked rubbing shoulders with kings and presidents and the upper class (and took on their habits, like smoking cigars and playing golf). The party dissolved itself a month after Haditu's decision.

You eliminated them all and became the sole standard-bearer of socialism.

```
        Three commit suicide in a single day:
     A 45-year-old man with a beard, wearing a white
        kaftan and a galabiyya, threw himself off the
     Abou el-Ela Bridge. A 17-year-old young man jumped
        into the Nile from the New Fontana Bridge.
     Another young man jumped from beside the Muhammad
     Ali Palace in Shubra; the ID card found on his
            body identified him as 23-year-old
                Nabil Jacques Hanna.
```

Egypt's Identity: A Study in the Genius of Place
by Gamal Hamdan.

15 April

Palestinian resistance officer killed in Amman.

75 years ago in Egypt:
A layman's guide to venereal disease—
We were given a copy of the book *Selections on Venereal Disease,* written by the illustrious Dr Mohamed Effendi Amin Badr, senior physician at the insane asylum. This major volume includes all current medical knowledge about these pernicious diseases and how to treat them.

Jordanian authorities foil attempted missile strike against Israeli port of Eilat.

American Cultural Center in Amman burns down.

18 April

Another Israeli attempt to penetrate into the Egyptian interior took place this morning when two Phantom planes took off towards Fayoum and were met by eight Egyptian MiG-21 planes. The Israeli directing officer came over the radio between the Israeli command and the Phantoms: 'Watch out. There is a trap waiting for you. Return as soon as possible.'

Enemy sorties on Egyptian targets in the first 4 months of this year average 180 per week.

75 years ago in Egypt:
French consular court in Cairo rules that the
Compagnie de Suez is a French company only and not
a joint venture.

Dad for Rent
New film with screenplay by Saad Eddin Wahba, the
deputy minister of culture.

Lenin Peace Prize awarded to Khaled Mohieddin,
chairman of the Egyptian Peace Council, and to
al-Shafie Ahmed al-Sheikh, general secretary of
the Sudanese Workers' Trade Union Federation.

19 April

Karim Mroueh, one of the leaders of the Lebanese
Communist Party, at forum held in Khartoum:
'Scientific socialism laid the groundwork for Arab
revolutionary thought.'

Protests force Mr Sisco to leave Beirut 4 hours
after arriving.

Attack on US Embassy in Beirut. American flag
burned.

Major strikes by Egyptian planes on enemy targets
from northern to southernmost positions.

Hassan al-Imam directs new film, *Dalal*, based on
noted writer Naguib Mahfouz's adaptation of
Tolstoy's novel *Resurrection*.

20 April

For the second time in 24 hours, Egyptian planes
strike enemy targets in Gulf of Suez.

Investigation reveals that dealer previously
owned 7 cinemas in Cairo including Ramses Cinema.
After they were nationalized, he worked in fake
antiquities and smuggled artefacts.

The Central Committee of the Socialist Union
celebrated the centennial of Lenin's birth with
Vice President Anwar Sadat and members of the
Supreme Executive Committee. The youth organization
held a conference for the occasion, attended by
Mr Diaa al-Din Dawoud, a member of the Supreme
Executive Committee, Shaarawi Gomaa, secretary
general of the Socialist Union, and Dr Mufid
Shihab, secretary of the youth organization.

The Marsh Snipes, a play.

Political organizations had always been a thorn in your side.
Since the beginning you'd been against party politics. You'd
seen how the main parties were led by the feudalists and capi-
talists who took orders from the palace and the British—except
of course for smaller nationalist parties, like Fathy Radwan's
New National Party and Ahmed Hussein's Socialist Party of
Egypt. There were also the secret communist organizations,
most of which came to view the army's activity as fascist or as a
military dictatorship of the kind that the US was sowing in Latin
America and elsewhere. When the leading parties rejected your
plan to set limits on agricultural land ownership—the long-
standing demand of the Egyptian people—you did away with
them and with party politics in general. You allowed the Muslim
Brotherhood to endure since you felt you might be able to use
their popular appeal to your advantage. Those hopes were
dashed when they tried to control you. You clashed with them

and dissolved their organizations. You figured you could gather Egyptians from different social classes in a single organization, the Liberation Rally, around a single goal: expelling the British. When that goal had been achieved you began to ask yourself: Well, now what?

You were the most knowledgeable of your colleagues, the most capable of developing your perspective, the most sensitive to the plight and the dreams of the poor. You were appalled by how British, French and Belgian companies and banks controlled the major Egyptian companies. The country's wealth was in the hands of a few foreigners along with some of the feudal families. In addition to huge shares in those companies, they owned vast amounts of land that they had not toiled to earn but rather had been granted to them by Muhammad Ali and his family. You could see a new stage of total social revolution taking shape. It was no longer just about bringing down feudalism and redistributing land to the fellahin, increasing wages for agricultural labourers, or doing away with titles like bey and pasha. You saw the importance of pursuing industrialization, electrification and building the High Dam. When the World Bank withdrew its support, you demonstrated outstanding courage and nationalized the Suez Canal Company. Foreign powers had dominated the Egyptian economy and its companies and banks, so you nationalized Banque Misr, which controlled 227 companies. Then you nationalized the major companies and established a public sector to manage national resources. This ensured that resources would be available for large-scale development projects to provide services as never before to the Egyptian people across many sectors: healthcare, food, education, transportation, housing.

But it was not long before you ran into difficulties carrying out all this. The administrative machinery of the state was controlled by the upper classes and the conservative right-wing, and you realized there was a need for a grassroots organization to counter them.

You were also aware that the Liberation Rally was in a vulnerable position: it had been taken over by opportunists, hypocrites and the feudalists' and landowners' cronies. You dissolved it and formed the National Union to create the cooperative, democratic society that you'd imagined, but quickly realized you were running into the same obstacles as before. The ideas were fuzzy. Gradually you came to understand that there was no way around staging a socialist revolution truly grounded in scientific principles—that is, in Marxist thought, without getting into the philosophical side, just the economic and social dimensions. You needed an organizational framework for this on the ground: the Arab Socialist Union.

You monitored the development of the Socialist Union, which had replaced the National Union. You could see it was dominated by family connections and traditional sources of power. It meant that your platforms had to appease conservative and regressive elements, like by switching between 'Islamic Socialism' and 'Arab Socialism'. Or the pointless discussions on 'revolution before development, or development before revolution?' and so on. The main thing was that the organization you'd wanted to be grassroots hadn't been able to mobilize the masses in the way you were personally capable of doing.

You watched the communists' successes with a mix of admiration and fury. They could organize themselves and work with the masses. You'd seen them do it many times, especially during the Tripartite Aggression, when they were actively involved in the popular resistance in cities occupied by the aggressors. In 1957, during the free elections for the National Assembly, you saw how they almost got one of their own into the assembly but didn't succeed because of internal divisions you successfully exploited. In any case, after this pantomime of democracy was over, they were brought before an emergency military tribunal.

You tried organizing the Socialist Union into groups led by individuals whom you particularly trusted: The youth organization was formed under the auspices of Zakaria Mohieddin, minister of the interior, while the wing responsible for ideology was put in the capable hands of Kamal Rifaat, one of the Free Officers. He was a hero of the popular resistance in the canal zone during the Tripartite Aggression of 1956. You considered him one of your most loyal men (until it later became apparent that he was actually more loyal to Abdel Hakim Amer). Ali Sabri, who became the head of the Socialist Union in 1966, was frustrated with this wing, which he felt was just trying to outdo the youth organization which had come to be led by his pediatrician, Hussein Kamel Bahaeddin. In the end, Shaarawi Gomaa spearheaded a huge police campaign in October 1966 to purge the Socialist Union of leftists. The detainees were questioned under torture, which began with being hung from an iron rack for several hours and then beaten with a stick to make them denounce Kamal Rifaat and the others. Meanwhile, you'd got the secret Vanguard Organization up and running with the help of Shaarawi Gomaa, who by then was also minister of the interior.

You wanted the Vanguard Organization to be an undercover group of the most devoted socialists. They were not allowed to own land or capitalist projects. You also excluded the communists, who were in prison. The first secret meeting was held at your home on 13 September 1963 and included Ali Sabri, Heikal (who was a dear friend, so you turned a blind eye to the industrial chicken farm he owned, as you also did with Zakaria Mohieddin), Abbas Radwan (who was later involved in the plot with Abdel Hakim Amer) and Ahmed Fuad (head of Banque Misr and a former communist). You all decided together that each one would recruit ten others who fit the above conditions and then those people would find ten more, and so on. Everyone recruited their followers and subordinates first and gradually started to make exceptions to the conditions. So it was that this secret Vanguard Organization contained most of the foremost administrative and executive officials in the country, including the sheikh of al-Azhar, the prime minister and the minister of the interior!

After the ghastly defeat of 1967 you realized you had to accept what you'd always tried to avoid: political pluralism and overt opposition. You figured it would be enough to have a party led by Abdel Latif al-Boghdadi and Kamal al-Din Hussein who were further to the right than you. Then, in the middle of your speech at a meeting of the Socialist Union leadership two months after the defeat, you said, 'They're both on our side anyway—they agreed to the charter. We'll permit them to form an opposition party and publish a newspaper.' Change only came from within that tight circle.

22 April

Egyptian Air Force strike enemy military camp on the Mediterranean coast.

Israel tries to seize Jordan's water supply.

Grand springtime soiree at the Rivoli Cinema
sponsored by the governor of Giza,
Mohamed al-Baltagi.

Tenth turbine activated in the Aswan High Dam
power station, raising electric energy production
from the station by half a million kilowatts
daily.

Newest summer 1970 styles from the
High Fashion Stores Company
Two-piece ensemble: *crêpe mousse* mini-dress
and maxi-coat in chocolat au lait with
embroidery on the chest.

23 April

Crisis heats up again in Lebanon.

Dramatic chase through the streets of Cairo
involving police and taxi thieves.

Palestinian youth recounts how he was drugged and
castrated by an Israeli doctor after he refused to
collaborate with Mossad.

Opening Monday in Cairo Cinema:
The Sicilian Clan.

25 April

1,600 British soldiers serve in the Israeli army.

Israeli Ambassador Yitzhak Rabin in Washington:
US Phantom and Skyhawk planes will be delivered to
Israel in secret.

Currently in press:
Believing in the Messiah
by Father Matta El Meskeen.

Lucrative trades in the Egyptian market: women's
hairdressing, truck rentals, the gold industry,
taxi cabs, selling sweets.

26 April

Egyptian units cross the canal three times
in under 21 hours.
Enemy sustains 35 casualties.

Military funeral for 3 martyrs from the Air Force:
An impressive national procession. Sister of
martyr Mohamed Saadallah refuses to be
photographed: 'Take photos of the heroes, for we
will not mourn or weep until we can join them.'

'Will I See You Tomorrow?'
A new song from Umm Kulthum
written by Sudanese poet Elhadi Adam
and composed by Mohammed Abdel Wahab.

Four new ministers for the Egyptian government:
Mohamed Fayeq, minister of state for foreign
affairs; Hassan al-Tuhami, minister of state; Saad
Zayed, governor of Cairo and minister of state;
Sami Sharaf, the president's secretary of
information and minister of state; and Mohamed
Hassanein Heikal, minister of national guidance,
replacing Mohamed Fayek, who had held the
post since 1966.
Hafez Ismail appointed director
of general intelligence.

Egyptian physician becomes first woman to attain
rank of first lieutenant in the army.

29 April

Enemy planes downed over Fayed.

White House announces it will agree to Israel's
request for more arms.

The story of the bridge began ten years ago in
1960 when the tender was awarded to the contractor
with the lowest bid. The following year, the state
discovered that this bidder had violated the
conditions of the contract, so the tender was
cancelled. The same contractor won the new tender
and failed to carry out the task in a timely
manner, so the ministry gave him a year to finish.
Since he had still not completed the project, it
was taken away and assigned to the state-owned
workshops. When they were unable to complete the
task, the ministry held another public tender in
early 1967. The job fell to a public sector
company that also failed to carry out the work
because the bridge project was placed under state
sequestration. The governor of Dakahlia was then
asked to formally appropriate the bridge project
since the bridge was government property. The
governor requested that the issue be resolved
amicably and that the contractor be given one last
chance. The ministry and the bidder came to terms
and the contractor was once again assigned the
project in November 1969. When still no progress
had been made during a five-month period, the
tender was permanently taken away from the
contractor and again given to the public sector,

which encountered the same issue with the
sequestration of the bridge, and so the project
was given back to the governor and the contractor
all over again!

Gratitude and regards to
the people and governorate of Qalyubiyya,
the secretary-general and members of
the Socialist Union, the governorate council and
all relevant agencies, and the workers in the
companies and factories in Shubra al-Kheima,
Abu Zaabal and al-Khanka.

30 April

Full Egyptian infantry battalion crosses the Suez
Canal by night with all its equipment and tears
down barbed wire and minefields set up by the enemy
around their positions, then returns to the west
bank of the Suez three and a half hours later.
3 soldiers were martyred and 7 wounded.

1 May

Abdel Nasser speaks to 20,000 workers in Shubra
al-Kheima on International Workers' Day: Without
Russian arms and support, Moshe Dayan could have
made it here to Cairo.

Electronics industry becomes self-sufficient and
prepares to begin exports.

Major expansion in electric cable manufacturing
for lighting projects powered by the
Aswan High Dam.

75 years ago in Egypt:
Prince Muhammad Ali Tewfik, heir presumptive and
brother of Khedive Abbas Helmi II, intends to
travel to Europe for the hot months of the year.
He will depart from port next Saturday or Sunday
on a French steamship arriving from China. May
Providence protect his journey.

2 May

US offensive in Cambodia encounters setbacks.

King Hussein in telegram to Abdel Nasser:
I will not hesitate to do what I must for the
Arabs' best interests.

Armed confrontation between resistance and
Jordanian forces near Shuna.

4 May

Egyptian attack by sea across Gulf of Suez targets
enemy positions in al-Tor.

Full bonuses for all state employees this month
despite the war, totalling 16 million LE.

New governor Wagih Abaza calls for greater focus
on keeping Cairo clean.

5 May

58-year-old taxi driver pulls over on Qasr El Nil
bridge and throws himself into the river.

Crisis continues between Jordanian authorities and
Palestinian resistance.

75 years ago in Egypt:
Lord Cromer and Boutros Ghali Pasha set to
exchange official visits on the birthday of Her
Majesty Queen Victoria. The citadel will hold a
21-cannon salute at noon that day.

Gaddafi convenes colloquium on revolutionary
thought in Libya.

First anniversary of the passing
of national martyr
Flying Officer Wagih Magli Georgy.

Soviet Union presents draft resolution to the UN
on the withdrawal of foreign forces from occupied
territory and stopping attempts to repress
national liberation movements.

3,000 Nasr 125 cars produced annually.
Nasr 1100 model changed to Nasr 128.

Colloquium on revolutionary thought headed by
Colonel Muammar Gaddafi concludes in Tripoli after
two days of discussion on determining the scope of
the working people whom the revolution serves.

7 May

UAR undertakes major military manoeuvre with live
ammunition and aircraft. President Abdel Nasser
monitors progress of the manoeuvre all day.

9 May

Israel attacks southern Lebanon.

Thousands rally in front of the White House to
protest the invasion of Cambodia.

Nixon on Cambodia:
'I could be wrong, but if I am wrong,
I am responsible and nobody else.'

10 May

Arab Sinai Organization destroys enemy
communication lines, captures a 4-tonne Israeli
trailer, and withdraws with it across the canal.

Israeli planes bomb southern Lebanon.

Central Committee of the Socialist Union,
headed by Anwar Sadat, meets to discuss the
organization's activities at home and abroad.

Moshe Dayan calls on Israeli settlers in the
Galilee to stand their ground despite
resistance attacks.

Sophia Loren and Marcello Mastroianni star in
Yesterday, Today, and Tomorrow
directed by Vittorio De Sica.

Jehan Sadat's Talla Society offers a simple meal
of feteer and mish at its fundraiser at the
Sheraton Hotel. Poet Souad Al Sabah, wife of
Sheikh Abdullah Mubarak Al Sabah, donated 500 LE
and two lambs roasted Kuwaiti-style.

13 May

Eastern front in flames after Israeli attack;
Syrian aircraft enter the fray.

Egyptian patrol destroys armoured enemy division
in Suez Canal crossing operation during the early
hours of the morning.

Abdel Nasser to US newspaper:
We'll need Russian technicians as long as the war
is underway. I've been writing to Brezhnev every
week for some time now. We have urgently needed
their support, weapons and technicians.
Before 1967, we had an army of 100,000 men—
now we have 600,000. Our defence budget was
160 million LE and now it's 550 million LE.
In 1967, we learnt to not be complacent and
not to assume that we know everything.

Bloody racial unrest continues
in US state of Georgia.
6 black people shot dead by police.

Dar al-Katib al-Arabi releases
A Guide to Emigration.

14 May

Aerial battle with Israeli planes over Bardawil
Lake.

Bombing in Gaza.
Resistance factions force Israelis to withdraw
from southern Lebanon. Violent clashes with the
enemy on the Jordanian front.

Kim Il Sung, the hero of the twentieth century:
Finally, the book you have all been waiting for—
the life story of the hero brought forth by Korea,
and the glorious saga of the revolutionary battles
and triumphs, outstanding leadership and lofty
virtues of the general who led the national
liberation struggle to victory, the likes of whom
have never been seen in the world before.
—*Paid advertisement*

16 May

That was the day in May 1967 when you made the first error in your calculations. You had asked the UN Emergency Force to withdraw from the border in Sinai, Sharm el-Sheikh and the Straits of Tiran. You re-established Egyptian sovereignty over the Gulf of Aqaba, which Egypt had lost in the Tripartite Aggression of 1956.

You moved the Egyptian forces to where the UN Emergency Force had been so that you could rescue Syria if Israel attacked. The enemy had played up this threat with help from their agents within the Syrian leadership itself. You should have taken that into account, expected it, but you didn't—even though you'd been warned that the Americans were trying to corner you. You gave Israel the opportunity that it had hoped for and it quickly moved its forces from the Syrian and Jordanian fronts to the Egyptian front.

Average enemy sorties over Egyptian positions reach 526 by second week of May.

Egyptian missile boat sinks Israeli vessel.

Resistance missiles hit enemy settlements in Jordan.

Le Monde:
Egypt receives Soviet MiG-21 aircraft.

29 pickpockets jump the train to Alexandria and rob passengers.

22 years since the founding of the State of Israel.

Bold attack by Egyptian frogmen on the
Port of Eilat.

Arafat: Battle of al-Arqoub demonstrates
Palestinian resistance's capabilities.

Egyptian planes launch 4 attacks in a day full of
aerial operations.

17 May

Israeli airstrike hits Egyptian destroyer docked
in port of Berenice on the Red Sea.
Egyptian aircraft downs 3 enemy planes.

Hafez Badawi, secretary of the general committee
for citizens' war committees, announced the
committees' plan of action yesterday, which will
be presented to the public for their suggestions
and feedback.

US Secretary of Defense:
We hope that the arms we've sold to Israel will
help it to exercise self-restraint in its
operations against Arab countries in addition to
bolstering its military capabilities.

Ben Gurion to *The Guardian*:
Israel will be at peace once Abdel Nasser's vision
for pan-Arab unity has been overcome. 'The end
of that dream will be the beginning of peace.
In eight or ten years there will be a
complete change.'

18 May

Egyptian destroyer sunk after clashes with enemy;
crew is rescued.

Enemy loses 5 planes in 24 hours.

Israeli aircraft strikes Jordanian positions.

20,000 feddans of new land to be distributed to
beneficiaries starting next July.

Unlikely network of 31 warehouse supervisors and
secretaries of agricultural reform cooperatives
engaged in misappropriation of fuel
and spare parts.

20 May

90 Egyptian soldiers cross the canal and destroy
armoured enemy column.

US magazine: In the last several weeks, the
Soviet Union has supplied Egypt with 16 Sukhoi
Su-7 fighter planes.

In a recent phone call, Sheikh Mohamed Saqr
Al Qasimi, ruler of the Emirate of Ras al-Khaimah,
denied accusations made by a Kuwaiti newspaper
that he had sold two islands in the Arab Gulf to
Iran in exchange for huge sums of money
and 20 luxury cars.

Israel bombs 70 houses in Nablus.

22 May

US sends 130 attack helicopters to Israel.

Iraqi consul in Bombay admits to shooting his
friend, the former Iraqi ambassador to Afghanistan,
with 7 bullets after the latter slipped sedatives
into his food while he was eating dinner, and then
along with 4 Indian guests violated him.

Resistance sets ambush for Israeli bus in
the Galilee.

US magazine: The US is the no.1 arms exporter
in the world.

Abdel Nasser, wearing short sleeves and
sunglasses, visits Suez and Ismailia during enemy
airstrikes; Israelis only 100 km away.

That was the day in 1967 when you announced that the Gulf
of Aqaba would be closed to Israeli ships, which was seen as a
declaration of war.

25 May

First anniversary of the victory of the Free
Officers' revolution in Sudan led by Major General
Jaafar Nimeiry.

From the lectures for the national and social
training course for diplomats:
'The Political Organization of the United Arab
Republic' by Shaarawi Gomaa.

People's Republic of China sends 474th warning to
the US for violating Chinese airspace and waters.

27 May

Lebanon asks Arab forces to help its army fend off
Israeli attacks.

Abdel Nasser and Gaddafi travel to Khartoum to
celebrate the first anniversary of the Sudanese
revolution.

President Nimeiry announces the nationalization
of British, US, Indian, Lebanese and Jordanian
companies.

28 May

Meetings between Abdel Nasser, Gaddafi and Nimeiry
continue in Khartoum.

Israeli Skyhawk downed.

Palestinian resistance attacks Israeli
settlements.

Secret meeting held between Yitzhak Rabin and
US State Department.

Visit Cairo's International Trade Fair
and don't forget to buy raisins for Ramadan,
Gianaclis olive oil, Ferro China Abu Simbel and
other products from the Egyptian Vineyards and
Distilleries Co.

Last US family leaves Libya's Wheelus Air Base
today, the largest US military base outside the
United States. Planes have departed on a
daily basis carrying several hundred civilians
and military families from the base (which cost
100 million dollars)—six thousand people in all.

Ramses Casino, al-Haram Street:
Sherifa Maher and Ahmed Ghanem.
Granada Casino: Safiya Helmi and troupe.
Arizona Casino: Soheir Zaki and Laila Gamal.

Industrial and Engineering Enterprises Co.:
High Dam, petroleum, water and sewage projects.

Florida
the Egyptian cigarette for all palettes
produced by El Nasr for Tobacco and Cigarettes.

Dr Aziz Sedky, minister of industry and petroleum,
in the tannery company's pavilion
at the Cairo International Trade Fair.

The Egyptian Real Estate Company, the United
Arab Maritime Company, the Egyptian Company for
Electric Equipment (Shaher), the Egyptian General
Organization for Spinning and Weaving
and its associated companies, and El Nasr Company
for Electric and Electronic Appliances (Philips).

Arabic subject examinations to be cancelled
next year in preparation for eliminating tests
and evaluating students based on their cumulative
work that year.

400 new buses exported to Iraq, Syria and Kuwait.

Qatar Media seeks musicians for radio and
television ensemble.

Prizes drawn for
Carnaval bathroom soap competition
produced by Tanta Company for Oil and Soap.

El Nasr Export & Import Co. announces
that Russian products are available.

First violinist Ahmed al-Hafnawi flies to Kuwait
tomorrow with Farid al-Atrash to record songs.

75 years ago in Egypt:
The Minister of Education and Public Works
requests that the Minister of Finance provide a

loan of 12,000 LE with 3.5 per cent interest from
the Public Debt Commission for agricultural land
reclamation in the Wadi estate, one of the areas
in Wadi Tumilat.

Nile Hilton Hotel announces opening of
Tropicana nightclub.

Nour Salem stores.

Arafa Interiors.

El Tahhan Co. for Irons and Metals.

Ramses Sheet Steel Factory.

Caliph al-Ma'mun private schools
in Manshiyat al-Bakri.

Ghabour Brothers.

Morcos
for Preserved Meats.

Atlas Stovetops and Ovens.

Fortieth anniversary of the passing of
First Lieutenant Ezzat Sobhy Askander and
First Lieutenant Mokhtar Youssef al-Radi.

First mosque for women built with 3 floors:
Abdel Ghani Mahmoud, educational superintendent
for Giza and the brother of Dr Abdel Halim
Mahmoud, general secretary of the Islamic Research
Academy, donated funds to build a 3-storey mosque
for women on a 1,000-square-metre piece of land.
The project will cost 50,000 LE and the
cornerstone will be laid by Dr Abdel Aziz Kamel,
the minister of Islamic endowments.

First anniversary of the passing of
Captain George Labib Tusa.

Egyptian engineer, age 27, studying at the
Leningrad Electrical Engineering Institute,
invents an electronic device for measuring
radiation emitted by generators.

Qatar's first cabinet since independence is formed
under the leadership of Prime Minister Sheikh
Khalifa bin Hamad Al Thani, the deputy emir. The
cabinet includes six members of the ruling family
and three Qatari citizens; Britain will oversee
the defence and foreign ministries.

Gaddafi: The fight against the enemy must be an
Arab national struggle.

Israeli newspaper reports that the Soviet Union
will provide the UAR with huge quantities of
landing gear, amphibious vehicles and weapons.

75 years ago in Egypt:
(1) The government has decided to grant the
Suarès foreigners and their companies a concession
to establish a water company in Tanta. We are well
aware of the integrity of the gentlemen who
received the concession but we do not feel that
the government is paying sufficient heed to a
matter that requires its attention, that is, not
to allow a monopoly of the sort that we have seen
with the water companies in Alexandria, Cairo
and elsewhere, which causes harm to
the general population.
(2) Annual celebration of the accession of the
British Queen Victoria held yesterday; Foreign

You could still recall the British soldiers in Cairo during the Second World War. They'd take off their shirts and stand bare-chested before the high windows of the enormous Qasr El Nil barracks, looking out over the Nile. The barracks were located in the same place where the Arab League building and Hilton Hotel would later be. The nearby Qasr El Nil Bridge led up to the statue of Saad Zaghloul. The following bridge, which is now known as al-Galaa'—Evacuation Bridge, after the evacuation of the British—used to be called the English Bridge (or sometimes Badia Bridge, after belly dancer Badia Masabni's nightclub). The whole area used to be British, with the Union Jack flying high. The embassy, barracks and Anglican Cathedral occupied a huge amount of space. Then there was the Gezira Club for the British forces and their families as well as the aristocratic Egyptian elites. All of the buildings in this area were red English-style buildings surrounded by tall European trees and complete with slanted roofs, even though it wasn't rainy in Egypt. In Garden City there were vast palaces where shiny black Rolls-Royces with their big silver headlights could be seen through the gaps in the iron gates.

Today on the radio:
'I'll Have a Soda' by Leila Nazmy
and
'The Washtub Told Me: Go Take a Bath'.

29 May

Abdel Nasser in Khartoum:
The Arab people have embarked upon a new life, a new birth. After the defeat of 1967 we asked the Soviet Union to send advisors and experts so that we could learn to use sophisticated electronic weapons. They sent us what we asked for. And now we have Soviet experts embedded in Egyptian units. They are with our forces everywhere. At the beginning of this year Israel developed a new strategy and began to strike the Egyptian interior—the outskirts of Cairo. It targeted schools and killed children. It hit factories and killed workers. With the help of the Soviet Union, we have been able to obtain modern weapons to prevent further penetration of Egyptian territory by Israel, which the US is supplying with Phantom and Skyhawk planes. The US played the same role in 1967 that France and Britain had in 1956.

Doxem
the most effective insecticide for cockroaches.

Stunning victory for leftist coalition leader in Sri Lanka's parliamentary elections: a decisive blow against colonial and Israeli involvement in South Asia.

Mr Anwar Sadat, vice president of the UAR, embraces President Abdel Nasser at the Cairo airport upon his return from Khartoum.

Metro Cinema presents:
A Race against Death.

A Man for All Seasons
starring Paul Scofield at Opera Cinema.

The Man Who Lost His Shadow
at Normandy Outdoor Cinema.
Top films of the season, every season.

Lotfy El Kholy no longer listed
as the editor-in-chief of the leftist *al-Tali'a*
magazine, which operates under Heikal.

You had listened to a recording from the intelligence agency at Lotfy El Kholy's house while he was hosting Nawal al-Mahalawy, Heikal's secretary, and her husband, who had been an officer under Abdel Hakim Amer. They started to talk politics and Lotfy's wife called you a dictator. Lotfy said that things were only going to change if they took matters into their own hands. You were angry because Lotfy himself had once called you 'the great fighter and mentor'. You ordered all four of them arrested. You cut Heikal off for a while but eventually relented. You thought about the power struggles within the regime and how various groups, especially the Socialist Union, Ali Sabri, the intelligence agencies and Abdel Hakim Amer, resented your close relationship with Heikal. It reached the point where two shots were fired at him when he left the al-Ahram building. You let them all go two months later, except Lotfy, who remained behind bars until your death.

Duty-free: Zodiac watches
that wind themselves automatically.

Grand opening of Sednaoui stores.

Egyptian Company for Pharmaceuticals celebrates
the prophet's birthday.

El Nasr Company for Wool and Fine Textiles (STIA).

General Company for Paper Industries (RAKTA).

Comprehensive screening of diabetes patients.

King-size Cleopatra cigarettes.

Sono Cairo Record Company presents:
Leila Mourad's 'The Light of My Eyes',
Laila Nazmy's 'Mama Na'ima' and Mohamed Qandil's
'The Flute and the Arghul'.

250,000 young men volunteer to serve
in 1,125 villages during the summer.

General Secretariat of Hafez Badawi's citizens'
war committees: General plan to be announced
within the week.

The Marsh Snipes, a play: Now in theatres.

For sale: Building in Dokki, 427 square metres,
two floors with four flats for 7,000 LE with an
instalment of 2,000 LE. New building in Shubra,
five floors, 12,500 LE with an annuity payment
of 810 LE.

Ferro China Romani Artichoke Liquor.

Chronograph watch, the choice of astronauts,
now available in Hanno stores.

Egyptian Tourah Portland Cement Co. announces job
vacancies.

For sale: El Nasr 1100 car, without license plate,
1,475 LE, final offer.

There are eyes everywhere——even among the
wheat and the rice.

Egyptian and Libyan ministers of industry
observe production at Nasr Company
for Steel Pipes and Fittings.

Anniversary of the passing of the martyr
Mohamed Mahmoud Ezzat.
Fortieth anniversary of the passing of
Major Fawzy Taha Qandil.

Director Naguib Surur receives year-long grant
from the Ministry of Culture for playwriting.

Governor of Cairo Wagih Abaza and Adel Gazarin,
president of El Nasr Automotive Manufacturing
Company, speak on syndicated radio programme.

Tonight on TV:
Anis Mansour's play *A Seat at the Table.*

30 May

Soviet statement: Israelis must be forced to
withdraw from the occupied territories.

11 resistance operations in the Jordan Valley
last night.

All Palestinian resistance organizations
(112 members in total) attend Palestinian National
Council meeting today in Cairo.

Duty-free: New Victory stainless steel
chronometer watches.

Huge discount on TVs of all sizes:
23-inch-screen TV for 140 LE
now only 134 LE.

Nixon accused of plotting to launch total war on
Cambodia to support Lon Nol.

Violent clashes continue between French police
and hundreds of leftist youth in the Latin quarter
of Paris.

Tonight at the Lycee El Horreya Theatre: *All in a
Twist,* starring Nagwa Salem.
Hosapir Theatre: Stand-up comedy
with Tholathy Adwa'a El Masrah.
Shahrazad Casino: Shokoko, Laila Gamal,
Souad Mekkawy.
Granada Casino: Safiya Helmi and troupe.
Arizona Casino: Soheir Zaki and Laila Gamal.
Le Perroquet Music Hall: Faten Farid.

Visit Cairo's International Trade Fair
Pavilions by Electro Cable Egypt, the Egyptian
General Organization for Electric and Electronic
Industries, and the General Company for Ceramic
and Porcelain Products.
Intercoms and PA systems from Benha for Electronic
Industries.

Koldair presents an economical new
air-conditioning unit.

General Company for Batteries
at the highest international standard.

25,000 subsidized SEAT cars to be produced
annually following agreement between Spanish SEAT,
Italian Fiat and French Renault companies.

Wages to be tied to productivity in public sector.

Modern Fashion Co. (Benzion, Adès & Rivoli) presents
the 6-ft Ideal fridge with a 5 LE discount
if purchased outright and a 4 LE discount
if paid in instalments.

Egyptian Sandstone Brick Co. in Cairo
offers red brick.

Reception held by al-Nour wa-l-Amal Association
for the ladies of the Arab and foreign
diplomatic corps.

Habiba (Gladys Abu Gawda) will act
alongside Farid Shawqi and Adel Adham in a film
directed by Hossam El Din Mustafa.

Dancer Zizi Mustafa and Puppeteer Shokoko return
from Africa.

Fouad el-Mohandes and his wife Shwikar sign
contract with theatre association for a play
directed by El Sayed Bedeir.

On this day in 1967—in a theatrical, almost farcical move—
King Hussein took his private jet to Cairo to announce to Abdel
Nasser that national duty had driven him to forget the past. He
declared his full solidarity with Cairo and expressed his desire
to form a joint command on the Jordanian front under an
Egyptian commander, Lieutenant General Abdel Moneim Riad.

You knew that Hussein was paid a million dollars a month by the CIA but you went along with it and let Abdel Moneim Riad accompany him back to Jordan. Two days later the chief of staff of the Jordanian army, Lieutenant General Khammash, met secretly with the US ambassador to Jordan and asked him to immediately move the twenty-five jet planes that the US had previously sent to Jordan outside the country until the present crisis between the Arab nations and Israel was resolved.

31 May

Egyptian units cross the canal twice and destroy
6 enemy armoured vehicles.
The battle lasted 7 hours and an Egyptian unit
crossed at Ras al-Ish and destroyed some of the
enemy's armoured forces.
Another Egyptian unit crossed from south of
al-Tina and destroyed one of the enemy's
armoured columns, which was on its way to rescue
the first group.
Enemy planes launched 400 sorties that night
over a 10-hour-period and expended 2,000 tonnes
of explosives.

Yasser Arafat presents a report on behalf
of Fatah to the Palestinian National Council
asking to form a unified leadership.

Residents of Arab Jerusalem refuse to pay
taxes to Israel.

Vietnamese revolutionaries occupy key city located
130 km north of Saigon.

Radio Cinema presents: Carlo Lizzani's
Revolutionary Titans (Requiescant).

Why do some immigrants return empty-handed?
They neglect to prepare themselves for the
unknown.

The National Folkloric Dance Troupe at
the Balloon Theatre.

Mandatory price controls placed on vegetables
this week.

Displaced persons from the canal cities
split into 3 groups; families kept together.

Duty-free: A poetic fragrance from Nina Ricci
L'Air du Temps.

El Nasr Company for Steam Boilers.

Lyndiol birth control pills from
Nile Pharmaceuticals.

General Company for Research and Groundwater.

75 years ago in Egypt:
(1) The French press drew attention to the
petition brought before the French Chamber of
Deputies by nationalist writer Mustafa Effendi
Kamil on behalf of many Egyptians, indeed on
behalf of all the people of Egypt, except the
traitors and turncoats among them, who are in
any case, a negligible few.
(2) Last shirt worn by Napoleon during his
exile in St Helena sold at a live auction in
Versailles, along with a lock of his hair and a
nail from his coffin.

1 June

Two enemy planes downed.
Israel concedes grave losses.
Fatah pays compensation to victims of Israeli
attacks on southern Lebanon.

Bourguiba returns to Tunisia after 6 months of
treatment in France.

Largest French nuclear test to date carried out in
Pacific Ocean.

Shortage of 17,000 sanitation workers in Cairo,
Giza and Alexandria.

Summer season begins in Ras al-Barr.

Now in stands:
June issue of *al-Tali'a* magazine.

Villa for sale in Heliopolis—will make a
grand residence.

Second anniversary of the passing of
Brigadier Mohamed Fathy el-Kholy.

8,000 pairs of shoes to be exported to
the Soviet Union next month.

Puppet Theatre to perform Yusuf Idris'
'Nuss-Nuss': The Miracle of This Age.

2 June

Resistance strikes Beisan with missiles.

Israel bombs Jordanian city of Irbid in the
northern East Bank.

Ruler of Umm Al Quwain—a small emirate in the Gulf—bans US company Occidental Petroleum from drilling in the Arab Gulf in territory contested between the emirates of Umm Al Quwain and Sharjah. Sharjah had granted drilling concessions to another US company which sought the aid of Britain as the power responsible for foreign policy in the two emirates to prevent Occidental from drilling. The disputed area is close to Abu Musa Island, which is currently under the aegis of Sharjah but sought after by Iran.

El Shorbagy Lino Fabric.

White Dacron Polyester.

Egyptian General Organization for War Factories: Factory 72 announces competition for open positions for employees and labourers.

Price of sterling falls to 2.39 dollars.

3 June

Enemy loses one Skyhawk as it carried out a raid on our positions in the Suez Canal at five o'clock in the afternoon yesterday and was met by our planes and air defence. Three of our men were killed and five wounded.

Britain provides Israel with military equipment.

Powerful earthquake in Peru levels entire cities and leaves 33,000 dead.

US sprayed toxic substances over residential areas in Vietnam on 40 separate occasions.

Opening night at Cairo Sheraton's Aladdin
Nightclub featuring belly dancer Nagwa Fouad.

8,000 tonnes of rebar produced for the
private sector.

Wanted: Janitor, salary 6 LE, and
female secretary with a nice appearance, 8 LE.
Wanted: 6-room luxury apartment in Zamalek—
willing to buy previous decor and furnishings.

Fortieth anniversary
of the passing of the hero and martyr
Squadron Leader Mohamed Abdel Gawad.
Fortieth anniversary
of the passing of the hero and martyr
Captain Mohammed Saad Abdullah.

First theatrical performance at a coffeehouse
in Attaba Square. The play was written by Nagi
George and directed by Mohammed Fadel.

4 June

3 enemy planes downed in battle over the canal.

Resistance operations in Jerusalem and the
occupied territories.

3 in every 100 Egyptian children at risk for
heart conditions.

New manufacturing agreement with the Soviet Union.

75 years ago in Egypt:
Yesterday Lord Cromer arrived from the capital and
in the afternoon was received in audience by
His Highness the Khedive to ask permission to

travel to Europe for his annual summer vacation.
He returned to Cairo this afternoon and will
travel from there to Port Said and sail on
the HMS *Coromandel* next Tuesday.

Ali Hussein expresses his thanks for condolences
for the loss of Lieutenant Hussein Ali.

Anniversary of the passing of
Flight Lieutenant Ahmed Radwan.
Anniversary of the passing of
Captain Essam al-Din Abbas.
Third anniversary of the passing of
Capitan Baligh Hussein Said.

The Iron and Steel Complex in Helwan: Soviet-Arab
cooperation in action.

Omar Effendi Stores offer rare chance for foreign
products sold in local currency: Philadelphia
cigarettes, Jordanian Hield wool (425 piasters
per metre).

5 June

Battles rage on all fronts with the enemy.
Funeral prayer in absentia for the June martyrs.
The president performs the prayer in Sayeda Zainab
Mosque.

Palestinian National Council forms military
command for the resistance.

Products from the Egyptian Vineyards and
Distilleries Co.

Nixon admits that 104,000 US soldiers have entered
Cambodian territory.

Israel announces that it has carried out 2,300
sorties on Egyptian positions since January 1970,
dropping 8,000 tonnes of explosives valued at
10 million pounds sterling.

Gaddafi goes to Baghdad, Amman, Damascus and
Beirut, asking, 'Why don't we have an eastern
front against Israel yet?'

US Justice William O. Douglas: McCarthy, Truman
and Johnson drove us to paranoia and policies of
suppression abroad; 'Our colleges and universities
reflect primarily the interests of the
Establishment...infiltration of CIA funds has
stilled critical thought'.

Incinerator in Alexandria destroys 3 million LE
worth of drugs.

Kuwaiti Sheikh Fawaz Al Sabah buys a lion cub from
the Giza Zoo for 100 pounds sterling.

Volkswagen car, 1965 model, 1,550 LE—final offer.

El Nasr Stores:
For a limited time only
Men's Tricoline pyjamas, 160 piasters
Children's Tricoline pyjamas, 75 piasters
Men's white Lino shirt, 175 piasters
Men's Cordonnet jacket, 160 piasters.

Residential building for sale: 16,000 LE with
annuity payment of 1,100 LE.

First anniversary of the passing of youth martyr
First Lieutenant Hisham Salama.
Third anniversary of the passing of the martyr
Captain Mahmoud Abdel Rahman al-Khadrawy.

Third anniversary of the passing of the martyrs
Lieutenant Colonel Mohamed Ezzat Abdel Hamid
First Lieutenant Walid al-Abadila
Captain Farouq Faris
Captain Mohamed Abdel Rahman Gomaa
Colonel Sayed Khalifa Qandil
Captain Farag Abdel Ghani Humam.

How you wished that day had never come! Those harrowing hours as the news came in. Looking for Abdel Hakim Amer without avail. Amer was in the air, at a loss. The lies pouring out of Radio Cairo. The Western media gloating. A chess game out of control. The trap had been well set: Operation Turkey Shoot, and you fell for it like a fool. Everyone laughed at your misfortune—in the papers in Beirut, even here in Egypt where the right raised its head and Sheikh Shaarawi said he'd thanked God for the defeat!

It had all lasted three and a half hours. At eight o'clock on the dot that morning the first wave of 174 Israeli planes carried out simultaneous airstrikes on all the Egyptian bases in the Nile valley, from Abu Suweir air base on the western bank of the Suez Canal all the way to the Luxor airport. That was followed by a second wave of 161 planes striking the forward airfields in the Sinai. Then there was a third wave of 157 planes that pulverized the rubble where the Egyptian airports and bases had been.

The Egyptian military command lost its nerve and the army was left stranded in the desert without any cover. That morning Abdel Hakim Amer had decided to go to the front, so orders were issued to hold anti-aircraft fire (though you had warned them about the impending Israeli attack). All of the army chiefs of staff and other commanders were there with Amer in the plane. (Some of them had served in the royal guard before the revolution, like Air Force Commander Sedky Mahmoud, while others had been involved in the fighting in 1956. Amer had insisted on retaining them in high-level positions.) The command at the front had been notified, as per usual Egyptian protocol, that the commander-in-chief was coming and most or perhaps all of them went to welcome the field marshal at the Bir Tamada air base to oversee the battle from there. These included the general commander for the front and the commander of the eastern region. The field marshal arrived at 8.20 and took off towards the Sinai five minutes later. When he neared the Abu Suweir air base, he saw the explosions on the main and secondary runways and heard reports over the radios that the Meliz and Kibrit airfields had also been hit. Another fighter plane in the air called out that it had been hit during take-off and needed somewhere to land.

As you said: All of this was happening as they flew over the Suez Canal and continued towards Bir Tamada air base. Lieutenant General and Air Force Commander Sedky Mahmoud asked the field marshal to go back, as their plane was still heading towards Bir Tamada. The commanders did not have enough information about what was happening but Abdel Hakim Amer went ahead and issued his decision from that plane. It was a very important decision . . . important but perilous, to execute the Fahd Plan—Operation Leopard—which involved a group of planes taking off from various air bases in order to strike several airports in southern Israel.

Abdel Hakim Amer arrived at Cairo International Airport, where no one was expecting him. The airport had just been hit and was in a state of chaos, when out came the commander-in-chief along with some other military men. They didn't find anyone waiting for them, so they took a taxi to the military headquarters in Abbasiya and asked Lieutenant General Mohamed Sedky Mahmoud to meet them there. He had been on his way to the Air Defence Forces' headquarters in Jabal al-Juyushi. Sedky Mahmoud and Abdel Hakim Amer both went to the army headquarters to look at what was happening. I think at this point he realized he was in a very difficult situation. He saw that the air force had taken a huge hit and that things weren't going well at all, but that nothing had happened yet to the ground forces in the Sinai. It occurred to him that the airstrikes might be the extent of it and he began to call the ground forces command. They all said to him that there had been skirmishes on the ground but nothing serious yet. That was how things looked at the time, but what was actually going on was something else entirely.

Meanwhile, you were in your office at home following the developments, thinking that the forces were ready. You'd told them what you thought was going to happen, that Israel was about to launch an air offensive. You later found out that as soon as you left the meeting, Abdel Hakim Amer had scoffed, 'How does he know that? Does he think he's a saint or something?'

At 9.30 a.m. you began to feel that the situation was much more serious than you'd realized. The reports coming in were garbled and incomplete. It was 12.30 p.m. and you couldn't wait any longer. You went to the headquarters near Abbasiya, where you found Hussein al-Shafei, Abdel Latif al-Boghdadi, Hassan Ibrahim, Kamal el-Din Hussein and some of the old guard from the Revolutionary Command Council, who had come to make sure everything was all right. You immediately sensed the general agitation and requested to see Abdel Hakim Amer alone. You asked him what was going on and at first he avoided meeting your eyes. He seemed to be trying to hide something that couldn't be hidden. He said that we'd been hit hard but that we'd hit back too, and that our forces were standing their ground even though they had no cover. He said that operations against the ground forces hadn't really even started yet. You weren't convinced. You pressed Amer to tell you the truth about the planes and the extent of the losses. Amer said that the airstrike had been bigger than Israel could handle, that there was another player involved.

You called Shaarawi, the minister of the interior, to ask him the truth about the downing of the Israeli planes. He confirmed the reports, but later it turned out they were actually just auxiliary fuel tanks that the Israelis had disposed of when they were done refuelling.

At 1.30 p.m. Shams Badran came into Amer's office and gave him a typewritten page, which he looked over and then handed to you. As you read, you realized the magnitude of the tragedy, the catastrophe that had befallen the ground forces, exposed in the Sinai without air cover. You snapped at Amer, 'Who are you talking about then?' He replied, 'The Americans.' You left Amer's office wanting to relieve him of his position and appoint a new commander-in-chief in his place, but abandoned the idea once you thought about the potential effect on the soldiers' good morale. It was just like in 1956 and 1961.

There was plenty of evidence of foreign involvement. On 3 June, King Faisal had tried to occupy the Tiran and Sanafir islands at the mouth of the Gulf of Aqaba, which were under

Egyptian control. During the following two days the Wheelus Air Base in Libya and the British bases in Cyprus hummed with activity. On the evening of 4 June, the British fleet command in Malta issued an order to its ships in the Mediterranean to join the US Sixth Fleet and receive orders from its command. Not to mention that Ralph Bunche, a UN undersecretary-general with close ties to the CIA, was behaving very suspiciously. And how did Israel have such detailed information about the Egyptian forces and their capabilities, far beyond the usual scope of reconnaissance? Some of our planes carried missiles and some didn't, and the Israelis always knew which was which.

6 June

Minister Pierre Gemayel, founder of the Kataeb Party, asks the Lebanese Council of Ministers to prevent Palestinian fedayeen from operating freely within Lebanese territory.

Madame Nguyễn Thị Bình, the Vietnamese revolutionaries' foreign minister, leaves Paris peace talks with US and returns to the struggle at home.

Price controls set for watermelon and grapes.

Arab States Broadcasting Union experts consider introducing colour TV.

Anniversary of the passing of
Major Mohamed Fathy.
Anniversary of the passing of
Major Medhat al-Melegy.
Anniversary of the passing of
Squadron Leader Mohamed Fathy Salim.

Anniversary of the passing of
Brigadier Negm al-Din Hassan.

Anniversary of the passing of
Brigadier Hussein Ahmed Rashad.

Anniversary of the passing of
Colonel Wadie Zaki Eskhayron.

Anniversary of the passing of
First Lieutenant Galal Anwar Behnawy.

Anniversary of the passing of
First Lieutenant Mohamed Adly Abdullah.

Anniversary of the passing of brothers
Colonel Mohamed Waguih Marei and
First Lieutenant Mohamed Safwat Marei.

It was at dawn that day in 1967 that Abdel Hakim Amer made the decision to withdraw. It was done haphazardly and by the evening of 8 June, there were 6,811 Egyptians dead.

That morning Amer had sent for the Soviet ambassador and accused him of colluding with the US. The ambassador said that the Security Council was considering a resolution for an immediate cessation of hostilities, but that the US had insisted that the resolution not include a withdrawal to the positions held when the fighting began. Amer agreed that the important thing was that the fighting stop immediately.

You called the Soviet ambassador the same day and told him that a ceasefire under the US conditions would constitute a victory for Israel, and that you needed new planes immediately because most of the Egyptian fleet had been hit on the ground. A few hours later, the ambassador replied that that his country would agree to Egypt's request for a large number of planes, but that the Soviets would prefer to send them in crates to Algeria and then ship or fly them from there to Egypt, to avoid provoking the United States.

The path to Cairo lay open before the Israeli forces, but they chose to occupy the West Bank and Jerusalem instead. By late evening a ceasefire resolution was passed but the Israeli forces continued their operations in the West Bank and Jerusalem. They encountered little resistance on the Syrian front and occupied the Golan Heights on the evening of 8 June. That night you made yourself write to King Faisal. You called on him to stand in solidarity as an Arab nation against this aggression and proposed holding an Arab League summit. Meanwhile, Amer announced to a group of his commanders that he was going to commit suicide and took his pistol into the bathroom next to his office. Several of his men jumped on him and snatched the gun out of his hands. Shams Badran called you on the phone and you rushed to the command headquarters. You begged Amer in a strained voice not to add oil to the fire. You told him you were convinced that it was all over. Amer burst out, 'It's not over yet.' You asked him wearily what was left then. Amer replied, 'The popular resistance.' Shams Badran agreed. Badran was always echoing Amer and even slept beside him in the same bed in the room adjoining his office. At that point Zakaria came in and stood there aghast, listening. You turned to Amer and asked him to join you in the room beside his office.

In the inner room, you informed him that you were certain you needed to resign from public life and that you wanted to announce your resignation to the country and appoint Shams Badran as the interim president. Amer seemed to agree, and then Zakaria, Anwar Sadat and Shams Badran joined you.

7 June

Statement issued by the resistance in Jordan
yesterday evening regarding the events in Zarqa,
24 km north of Amman.

Amman cut off from the outside world; exchange of
fire in the streets of the capital.

Resistance attacks settlements in the Galilee.
Israeli electrical lines destroyed south of
the Dead Sea.

US gives Thailand 200 million dollars to recruit
10,000 soldiers for the war in Vietnam.

400,000 Egyptian students begin taking their
secondary-school exams.

Trial for negligence in passenger train derailment
that resulted in 8 deaths and 9 injured.

Third anniversary of the passing of
Colonel Mostafa Tawfiq
Captain Essam al-Din Shakir
Captain Ali Hassan Salama, surgeon
and Captain Samir Abbas Mohamed.

8 June

Brutal clashes in Jordan between the
resistance and the army.
Skirmishes between resistance patrol and
Jordanian armed forces near Zarqa.

Fatah warns of plots to drag freedom fighters
into peripheral struggles.

Israeli helicopters attack Bedouin encampments
in Jordan.

Two Israeli airstrikes on southern Lebanon.

Largest defence budget in Egyptian history:
553 million LE. In 1967 the army's budget
was 160 million LE.

Egyptian artillery downs Israeli Skyhawk east of
Port Tawfiq.

US Secretary of State Rogers announces that Nixon
has decided to give Israel more Phantom and
Skyhawk planes in a new deal.

Brazil defeats England in the World Cup.

US army command in Vietnam announces loss of 3
helicopters downed by revolutionaries' artillery.

Steel complex completed a year early.
2,000 workers now employed at the plant with plans
to increase labour force to 120,000
within 2 years.

Production of Ramses cars halted. Factories shift
to producing microbuses.

86 merchants in Alexandria concoct matchstick
crisis.

Nile General Company for Reinforced Concrete
helps establish the Iron and Steel Complex.

Anniversary of the passing of national martyr
Pilot Officer Zuhair Shalabi.
Anniversary of the passing of
Pilot Officer Wafiq Ahmed Toulan.

Pay a piaster to sit in the same chair where
Field Marshal Rommel sat during the North African
campaign. The chair was found by a Greek
coffeeshop owner when Rommel left Marsa Matrouh
in 1942.

9 June

Efforts to rein in crisis between resistance and
Jordanian army continue. Clashes leave 104 dead or
injured. Resistance detains 40 Jordanian Special
Operation Forces involved in the clashes.

Egyptian defence fights off 24 Israeli Phantom
planes trying to strike Egyptian targets during
a 3-hour period.

Arafat elected commander-in-chief of the
resistance organizations.

10,000 Egyptian teachers return home from
working abroad in Arab countries, laden with fine
wool rugs and foreign currency.

Those five days—5 to 9 June 1967—were the worst in your life. Some moments were closer to waking nightmares. You spent most of that dark time lying in bed defeated, enervated, the crowd waiting outside. The ministers and men of state crowded the house, some even sitting on the stairs. You could hear them crying. The pain in your legs became worse and the sedatives and anti-depressants brought no respite, not even a few hours of decent sleep. As soon as you closed your eyes, you would see them: thousands of Egyptian soldiers rushing forth in the desert exposed, scores of Israeli planes hunting them down, shooting them one by one. You took out your pistol and placed it by your side. You thought of killing yourself but you didn't want to be compared to Hitler or Rommel. You'd always believed you were stronger than that.

At 7 a.m. on 9 June, Heikal arrived with the resignation speech. It was another calculated risk—a referendum of sorts, the outcome opaque. Would the people stay the course or forsake you entirely?

You had been in your office since dawn. You looked exhausted, like the years had suddenly caught up with you. If Amer had lost the army through his negligence, you were responsible. You were the one who had kept him by your side despite his shortcomings. Since the beginning he'd trusted you as his friend and brother, even a father, and you'd grown closer during the siege of al-Faluja in Palestine. His gentle demeanour and perhaps also his well-to-do background had made an impression on you.

You thought you'd leave the presidency to Shams Badran to mitigate the impact of your resignation on the army and the people. But you recoiled at the idea of leaving the country to Amer's feeble and corrupt men. Heikal added that it would seem like you were rewarding the army command responsible for the defeat—it would add insult to injury. You immediately concurred. The alternative was Zakaria Mohieddin, one of the original Free Officers and the first head of the General Intelligence Directorate. He was a thoughtful and level-headed man capable of dealing with the Americans because of his right-wing tendencies and animosity towards the Soviet Union. At least that was how you felt at that moment: Everything was lost and you needed to act accordingly.

The hours ticked by slowly that morning of 9 June. The news reports were saying that the military command had fled at the first opportunity and that 170 Egyptian planes had been completely destroyed. There were 11,000 dead, 500 officers and 500 soldiers taken prisoner, and 16,000 soldiers and officers missing in the Sinai. Some of these men made their way to Egyptian positions west of the canal in a wretched state. Injured soldiers spoke of companions they had left behind, bleeding out in the sand. You tried to not visualize this and realized bitterly how easily you had fallen for the trap. You felt utterly alone, in a way you had never felt before. Your thoughts returned to your decision to resign and have Zakaria Mohieddin take your place. You had never imagined for an instant that Zakaria would be the one to succeed you—Abdel Hakim Amer was always the one who came to mind.

Heikal asked for permission to go to Sami Sharaf's office to work on editing the resignation speech and replacing Shams Badran with Zakaria Mohieddin.

He walked over to the building opposite, where he found Sami Sharaf in a state of great agitation. Sami cried aloud when he read the speech stating you'd resign and leave 'my colleague, friend and brother Zakaria Mohieddin to assume the position of the President of the Republic'. Heikal returned twenty minutes later with a full draft of the speech. You asked him to read it aloud for you to get comfortable with it. Heikal read and you estimated it would last about twenty minutes—it would feel long. You told him that this was going to be painful for you and for the people.

It occurred to you that Amer was going to be surprised to hear Zakaria's name instead of Shams Badran's. He'd think you had deceived him with one of your classic manoeuvres and that you'd been bent on picking Zakaria all along and had only said Shams Badran to mollify him.

At 3.30 p.m. Heikal was going to leave you to rest a little before the speech. You asked him to stay with you if he didn't have something urgent to do. At 5 p.m. you glanced at your watch and asked if he wanted to go with you to al-Qubba Palace for the speech. Heikal apologized and said he would not be able to bear it. You were overwhelmed with feeling. You told him he'd been closer than a brother to you and that you didn't know what was going to happen tomorrow or whether you'd meet again.

You spoke earnestly about the friendship that had grown between you. Then you broke off and came back to the matter at hand: After you returned from giving your speech, you'd come back to your room and shut yourself off entirely from the people and the world. You asked him to look after everything that would be written or broadcast in your name until Zakaria was able to take the oath tomorrow before the National Assembly and formally assume office.

You shook hands and were unable to entirely hold back the tears in your eyes.

At 7 p.m. the car took you to al-Qubba Palace nearby. Half an hour later you could hear the military fanfare on TV. You went up to the microphone and began to read. Then it was over.

You went home utterly drained. On the way back you could see there was a strange commotion in the streets between al-Qubba Palace to Manshiyat al-Bakri, which were usually empty in the evenings.

You got out of the car and went into the house. Everyone around you was wailing and weeping. The guards and aides were all crying.

You went up to your room and sat down in your favourite armchair to think over what had just happened. You tried to imagine what the future would be like now that you had resigned. Would you have to leave this house, the only place you'd lived since it all began? Or would they let you keep it as a token of your service? What would your life be like? This was all you knew. Would you join Heikal and Zakaria in raising chickens? How would you live, when you only had a few hundred Egyptian pounds, no land or property? How would it go with the Socialist Union? Would you become a member of a committee led by one of your current subordinates? Or maybe you'd become a mechanic like comrade Badr?

Suddenly you heard air sirens. You didn't move and didn't pick up the telephone receiver to find out what was happening. You sat staring blankly at the phone in silence.

You couldn't speak, even to your wife who looked terribly worried and informed you there was quite a crowd outside the house. Around midnight you got yourself together, picked up the receiver and called Heikal. When he answered, you asked him wearily, 'What happened?'

He said that the government had moved to Sami Sharaf's office across the street, and that there were huge crowds around the house on all sides. Shaarawi Gomaa and some of the others were worried that something awful was going to happen, because the crowds seemed completely out of control.

You asked Heikal, 'What do they want?' He said, 'I don't know. They aren't demanding anything. They're just chanting your name over and over.'

Your heart raced. You looked at the pistol. Suddenly you felt the force of the furore nearby, the voices shouting, the cries of anger. In the same instant you saw a fuming Amer in your mind's eye, then Marie Antoinette when they came to lead her and her children out to the guillotine, and the tsar of Russia and his family executed, and Lumumba and Sukarno . . . Had your time come, too? Then several men pushed their way into your room despite efforts to hold them back. It was your top aides. They told you what was going on in a state of great distress. You took a breath and helped calm them, and then went down to your office. They followed but you asked them to leave you to evaluate the situation on your own.

You looked through some of the news reports and cables coming in. The first thing you read was a United Press cable about the shock dealt to the Asian and African delegations to the UN: Some had openly wept. Then you read the statement from General de Gaulle, the president of France who would resign two years later following a popular referendum (he would die two months after you). De Gaulle had said: We hope that President Gamal Abdel Nasser will have the courage and patriotism to respond to the sentiments of his people, who are asking him to stay in office. Then there was a slew of other cables about the masses of people crying in all the cities and villages throughout the Arab world. There was a cable describing how Lebanese President Charles Helou had burst into tears. You were told that Iraqi President Abdul Rahman Arif was on the telephone from Baghdad and when you picked up the receiver, he was weeping,

'I implore you, in the name of the Iraqi people and of pan-Arabism, to stay.' After that Ismail al-Azhari, the president of Sudan, called to say that Khartoum was going to boil over if you didn't relent and reconsider.

Reports began to come in from all over Egypt that huge numbers of people had swarmed the railway lines and taken control of many of the trains and any cars they came across, and that they were advancing on Cairo.

All the news from the front was the same: Grief had descended upon the officers and soldiers. In Ismailia, Port Said and the Suez, most had gone out into the streets wailing and chanting your name.

You called Heikal on the phone and asked him the question that was gnawing at you: Why? You couldn't believe what was happening. Heikal said that the National Assembly had been convened and had decided to continue the sit-in rejecting your decision to resign. Sadat—the Assembly's president—urged you to come.

You asked him what you should do. He said it was up to you, and you said you couldn't go back on your word now.

You left your office and went up the stairs to the second floor. You felt like you were sleepwalking, barely conscious of anyone around you. You went into your bedroom, changed your clothes mechanically and lay down on the bed.

At 12.30 a.m. you called Heikal and told him you were exhausted and that you desperately needed to rest. He advised you to take a sleeping pill, so you did but you still couldn't sleep. Your body was sleeping but your mind was still awake.

At 5.15 a.m. you gave up trying to sleep and called Heikal again and found he was awake too. You asked him if he might be able to come to you at that hour.

When Heikal left his home near al-Galaa' Bridge, the roads were still packed with people, despite the early hour of the morning. It was almost impassable. He went to his office in al-Ahram and called you to let you know the road was blocked and you replied, 'How strange the people are.' You had thought they'd want to hang you in Tahrir Square but quite the opposite was happening and you suggested it might be better for Heikal to remain at his office so you could reach him at any time.

You left your bedroom without changing your clothes, went down the stairs slowly and walked over to your office. The staff and guards didn't seem surprised to see you in your pyjamas. Most of them were red-eyed from crying and lack of sleep. You could hear voices in the dining room, so you went to go see. You found your wife and some of the children gathered around the table eating breakfast. A terrible silence fell as you went to your usual chair at the head of the table. One of them tentatively said, 'Good morning, Daddy.' You didn't answer. You drank the cup of tea your wife had just poured. She said something you couldn't hear—her voice was drowned out by the strange commotion outside. Chanting, but you couldn't make out the words. Suddenly Khalid left the room. The people seated at the table made halting, bland conversation, but you didn't join in.

Khalid came rushing back and said, 'Baba, the people want you.'

You replied sharply, 'That's none of your business.'

Your wife said, 'We're with you, for better and for worse.'

You didn't say anything. No one spoke a word.

You got up and left the room and went to your office, where you stood paralysed, looking at your desk. There was a stack of papers that had just been put there. You ruffled through them, your mind elsewhere. A message from U Thant, the UN secretary general, caught your attention. He had said: 'The secretary-general is concerned you have made this decision solely out of pride. He would like to remind you of the Buddhist saying that true greatness lies in the power to withstand adversity. He implores you to reconsider your decision, lest you unwittingly fall for a gambit others have played.'

You found that another message had come in from de Gaulle: 'Victory and defeat must take their turns in the history of every country; what matters is your strength of will. Half of France was once under direct occupation by the Nazis, as you may remember, and the other half was a puppet state. But France did not lose her will and stayed the course with her leaders who remained true. Courage lies in overcoming these tribulations, for happier times do not require such mettle. The Arab world needs you for peace. I will not hesitate to agree that the present state of affairs will not provide a solid foundation for peace.'

There was an even stronger missive from the Soviet troika opposing your resignation and expressing their willingness to alleviate Egypt's economic and military difficulties at any time.

You pulled yourself together and went up to your bedroom. You lay down on the bed and tried again to sleep, to no avail. You spent the rest of the day lying there, avoiding either food or conversation.

At 8 p.m. you rang Heikal again and told him that for the first time in your life you found yourself unable to make a decision and that you were getting ready to go to the National Assembly. Even if you managed to make it there with the crowds, you didn't know what you would say.

You hung up the phone and refused to pick it up again. You lay there brooding and thought about the crowds outside. Was it just a hysterical response to the shock? Rage? Or were they also trying to say something along the lines of what Abdel Halim Hafez would express in a famous love song: 'What has bound us will also set us free.' Yes: the message was for you to get up and get us out of the mess you'd made with your foolishness and vanity.

By the time ten o'clock came you had made a decision.

You picked up the telephone receiver and were told that Cairo was boiling over and that the roads to the National Assembly were all closed, filled with crowds that no one could control. Heikal suggested that you address the speech to the National Assembly instead of physically going there and you immediately agreed. You discussed the contents of the speech together and Heikal asked for fifteen minutes to write it before he called you again to talk over what he'd written. The speech was as follows:

Mr Chairman of the National Assembly:

I had been hoping that the people might help me in carrying out my decision to resign . . . No one can imagine how I am feeling right now given the astounding position that our people and all peoples within the great Arab nation have taken in refusing to accept my resignation . . .

I urge you to inform the distinguished members of the National Assembly that I am firm in the reasons for which I have made my decision. At the same time, the voice of our people is something that cannot be ignored. I have, therefore, determined that I will stay in office . . . until we are together able to remove the consequences of the aggression.

And then that part of your saga was over.

Al-Qahira Company for Agricultural Food Products and Fragrances.

General Nile Company for East Delta Buses.

Egyptian Chemical Industries (KIMA) of Aswan.

220,000 workers from the Egyptian General Organization for Spinning and Weaving pay tribute to the popular uprising of 9 and 10 June.

Water utilities hooked up to buildings constructed in violation of code.

Superintendents in the governorates authorized to extend secondment for teachers to work in private schools for periods longer than 2 years.

Third anniversary of the passing of the martyr First Lieutenant Kamal al-Din al-Desouqi.
Third anniversary of the passing of Flight Lieutenant Samir al-Aghuri.
Third anniversary of the passing of Captain Esmat Ahmed Talaat.
Third anniversary of the passing of Captain Samir Abbas Mohamed.

First anniversary of the passing of
Captain Hussein Lotfy.

Goodbye imported perfume—
Hello Favori Chabrawichi.

10 June

Crisis erupts again in Amman as fighting spreads
from outskirts throughout the capital.
Communications to Amman cut off.

Radio Amman:
Shots fired on the king's motorcade as he
travelled to his summer villa 14 km north of
Amman.

Yasser Arafat flew from Cairo to Amman and arrived
yesterday at dawn in the middle of the fighting.
Clashes began at 2 a.m. when Jordanian army units
attacked a resistance base. Around 9 a.m.
Jordanian forces attacked the Palestinian armed
resistance's command centre, inflicting
casualties. The resistance erected roadblocks in
the streets and barricaded themselves in a house
overlooking the commercial centre.

70 Israeli planes attempt airstrikes on
Egyptian targets yesterday from 1.15 p.m.
until 9.30 p.m.

Alexandria Royal and Nadler Confectionary Company.

Mela Mustafa al-Barzani, leader of the Kurdistan
Democratic Party, met today in northern Iraq with
Iraqi officials led by Saddam Hussein al-Tikriti,
vice chairman of the Revolutionary Command

Council, and Hardan al-Tikriti, the
vice president of Iraq.

BiscoMisr: Egyptian Company for Foodstuffs.

National Cement Production Company.

Egyptian Company for Wood Industries.

First anniversary of the passing of
Lieutenant Colonel Kamal el-Didi.
First anniversary of the passing of
Lieutenant Khalid Ismail.
First anniversary of the passing of
Major Mustafa Fouda.

11 June

Yesterday at noon Jordanian armoured divisions
attacked the al-Wehdat Palestinian refugee camp.
At 6.45 p.m. Jordanian artillery began shelling
all Palestinian areas of the capital.
Resistance forces issued a communique accusing
elements within the Jordanian government of
escalating matters to a breaking point,
particularly Major General Sharif Nasser, the
king's uncle and commander-in-chief of the army,
Major General Rasoul al-Kilani and
Brigadier General Sharif Zaid ibn Shaker.
The fighting began hours after an agreement was
reached between King Hussein and the resistance
organizations on how to resolve the crisis.
600 injured or killed today.
Power outages continue after bombing of
main power station in Amman, which is in a
complete blackout for the second day.

Abdel Nasser and Gaddafi discuss recent developments.

Production of Ramses automobiles is up to 900 cars this year and in two years will reach 3,000 cars.

Steel imports halted to promote domestic production.

12 June

650 wounded and killed during two days of fighting between Jordanian and resistance forces.

Gaddafi to the Egyptian National Assembly:
I see this as an inevitable result of the Arab left's excesses, which have reached an obsessive and treasonous level in the east, and of the Arab right's treachery and perfidy in the west. That is why one of the slogans of the al-Fateh Revolution in September was 'Neither left nor right' . . . and so I say: Yasser Arafat and Fatah are innocent. They did not set off civil war in Jordan and King Hussein is not to blame for this either.

Abdel Nasser to the Egyptian National Assembly:
The Palestinian resistance and Fatah in particular is one of the most important manifestations of our struggle, yet we cannot be oblivious to the errors that may have been committed by some of the resistance organizations. We cannot sit back and watch what is happening in Jordan. We know that both King Hussein and our brother Yasser Arafat have made efforts to reach a ceasefire.

Arafat responds to Abdel Nasser and Gaddafi:
We have made multiple agreements with our brothers
in the Jordanian government and the goal has
always been to reach a ceasefire and end the
unrest. But there are double agents still fanning
the flames of war and doing everything they can to
escalate the situation. This has reached the point
where they are ordering artillery tanks and other
forces to raze entire neighbourhoods in Amman and
Zarqa and targeting innocent, unarmed civilians.
Amman has become the theatre of operations—
operations that should be launched against Israel.
In the name of my brothers, I call on you in this
critical hour to do everything in your power to
stop the bloodbaths that these collaborators are
committing against our people.

Libyan flag flies over the
Uqba ibn Nafi (Wheelus) Air Base.

Leaders suspected of conspiring around events in
Jordan: Major General Nasser bin Jamil,
commander-in-chief of the army; Major General Zaid
ibn Shaker, commander of the Third Armoured
Division; Mohammed Rasoul al-Kilani, 'the man
behind the curtain', as they call him in Jordan,
and who was dismissed as director of general
intelligence in May 1968 and ejected from the
Ministry of the Interior during the crisis of
February 1970; and former Prime Minister Wasfi
Tal, known for his ties with the British but who
in the last three years has begun to develop a
radical nationalist agenda.

16 June

Two enemy planes downed. Direct hit explodes one
plane mid-air.

Prisoner exchange between the resistance and
Jordanian government after clashes in which more
than a thousand people were injured.

Jordanian army fires on helicopter carrying Arafat
before it lands at Amman Airport; pilot injured
and Arafat jumps from the plane.

Tenth anniversary of the passing of
Shuhdi Atiya al-Shafi'i,
who was martyred in Abu Zaabal Prison.

Nationalization of 6 oil companies in Algeria.

You made a surprise visit to the front in the early morning and joined the soldiers for breakfast in the trenches: hot lentil soup, cheese and tea. You sat on the ground among the officers and soldiers: Saleh, age 30, an artillery officer with a business degree from Damietta. Girgis, an educated farmer from Deir Mawas. Hashem, age 24, a graduate from the faculty of sciences, newly married last week. Abdul Raouf, age 24, an artillery officer, preparing for his thanawiyya amma exams. Sabry, an agronomist who graduated in 1967, now a primary-school teacher in Qena. All these educated young men, new fodder for the army.

Eleven o'clock in the morning: the siren sounds. Enemy airstrikes. Twelve o'clock: a group of enemy planes strike, then clash with the air defence systems. A barrage of heavy artillery fire. The planes retreat. Another air-raid warning at one o'clock.

Your aides were on edge and they insisted that you needed to leave immediately, lest the tragedy of Lieutenant General Abdel Moneim Riad repeat itself. He was hit by an enemy mortar while monitoring the front lines. You conceded and went back to following the updates from your office and bedroom over the telephone as the Israeli planes approached the Egyptian positions. Three o'clock: Missiles falling on the sand. Silence. One group with anti-aircraft artillery at the ready, another sleeping. You dozed off for a while too, until your aides called.

Your mind wandered as it always did when you were thinking about the trenches and the front. Was there something that had bothered you about the morning's visit? What was it? Yes—that photo of Che Guevara you'd seen hanging in the trenches. The CIA had killed him in Bolivia in October 1967. He was a strange kind of revolutionary and it had taken you a while to understand him. Overly romantic. He preferred the trenches of war to the halls of power and had captured the imagination of youth around the world. Like you once did, a decade ago.

You had met Che when he came to Cairo in 1965. You immediately sensed that he wasn't in good spirits. He left for ten days, some of which he spent in the Congo. When he returned, he told you that he was discouraged by what he had seen and that he was thinking of joining the struggle and leading two Cuban battalions there.

He said to you, 'We need to do more for revolution in the world.'

You replied, 'You're quite something. But if you want to become another Tarzan, a white man barging into an African struggle to lead and protect them, that's not going to work.'

As you talked together, you began to understand his disillusionment. He said he had great respect for Castro and considered him a brother and mentor, but that some things had happened between them that weren't quite right. First, Che had won Raul Castro over to communism while he was in Mexico without telling Fidel about it. Then, Raul joined the Communist Party and they decided to conceal it from Fidel. When he finally got wind of this he flew into a rage, both because of what had happened and because they had hidden it from him.

In any case, Castro got over his anger and made Che minister of industry. But that was an incredibly difficult role and Cuba, like everywhere, was dealing with serious problems. Che told you, 'We lost our way—maybe I'm to blame for that. We nationalized 98 per cent of what we had, even the barber shops, and then realized we were going to have to leave some people out.' He added that the people who were supposed to manage these nationalized institutions had forgotten their revolutionary fervour and turned instead to the embrace of their charming secretaries and luxury cars, their special privileges and air-conditioned offices and houses. They closed their doors in the face of the people just to keep the air cold, instead of letting the workers inside.

The conversation turned again to the Congo and you said, 'The first thing you need to do is to forget all about this idea of going to the Congo, because you won't succeed. I've already been through that in Yemen. When the revolution began there, I sprang to their aid—even though the reports indicated that the time wasn't ripe for revolution. I soon discovered, one, that you cannot shape a revolution from the outside, and two, that it's a long and torturous path. We can rush through the historical course of revolution but we cannot bypass the organic process that gives revolutions their power.'

You invited Che to come with you the next day to the opening of a new factory in a governorate near Cairo. On the way there you said to him that the romantic stage of revolution begins with unbridled passion. The day the revolution erupts is the day its romantic ideals come true. Its wedding night. But after the wedding you have to make the marriage work. You have to earn a living and put a roof over your head and start a family. That's what revolution means. It meant shouldering that heavy burden inherent in building factories and undertaking land reform, and turning that unrestrained fervour into an energy focused on specific plans and goals.

On the way there, you received a splendid welcome. In the villages, the families all rushed out, young and old, to greet your motorcade. People stood in front of your car and tried to stop it. Thousands came to cheer for you in that factory. Che was moved by this and said, 'This is what I want. This is the revolutionary spirit.'

At the end of the meeting, Che told you that he didn't think he was going to stay on in Cuba. He said that he hadn't determined yet where he would go and that he just had to decide 'where he could find a place to fight for global revolution and meet death head on'. And he did. He met his end a few months after your defeat in 1967.

You shook your head. It was a shame, for he was a man you'd liked from the outset. You put aside a certain pang of jealousy that you felt seeing your soldiers put up his picture beside yours. You went back to following the developments on the front, minute by minute from the trenches. At nine o'clock that night: a pass in review before the commander. Ten o'clock: a warning—a line of the enemy's armoured vehicles was bringing reinforcements to the troops that had been hit that morning. All at once the roar of artillery fire burst through the enemy lines. At eleven twenty-five, the fighting stopped.

```
       16 Kuwaitis from the Yarmouk Brigade killed
     during Israeli airstrikes on the west bank of the
                         Suez Canal.

                  Five bloody days in Jordan.
         Committee decides to halt printing of two
      newspapers for an indeterminate period of time:
             the Palestinian al-Difa', and al-Dustour.
        The decision was made at the request of King
       Hussein after both papers published a statement on
        8 June from the resistance's central committee
                  attacking the royal family.

      Dispute between a Muslim father and Christian
      mother regarding their son's inheritance. Court
       rules for the father because a child with one
       Muslim parent is under that parent's custody.
```

18 June

You flipped through the photo album: There you were, raising the Egyptian flag after the evacuation of the last British soldier on 18 June 1956. The memory filled you with pride: You had put an end to 70 years of colonialism. You turned the page to another famous photo from 1956, when you went to al-Azhar and declared: 'We will fight. We will fight.'

19 June

Al-Sanhuri, Youssef Wahbi and Naguib Mahfouz win
State Appreciation Awards.

21 June

Uneasy calm in Amman after Arafat's central
committee for the resistance announces that it
expects to clash with the Jordanian authorities,
particularly while King Hussein is away.

Joint vehicles for the resistance and army roam
through the streets of Amman to maintain the
peace.

Sukarno dies at his home in the Indonesian
capital, where he had been under house arrest
since General Suharto came to power in a US-backed
right-wing military coup in 1967.

You thought: Sukarno's tragedy was that he always played different sides off each other. That was the policy he had long pursued. In the end, the army controlled everything from football to public transport but neglected its main job of defending the country's borders. Was that your tragedy, too?

June was a strange month. That same day Napoleon returned defeated from Waterloo, and the following day he abdicated for the second time. He had said, 'Frenchmen . . . I offer myself as a sacrifice to the hatred of the enemies of France . . . My political life is over.' It was a story worth returning to. He took off the first consul's military coat and put on civilian clothes, and France experienced stability and peace for a short while. But his ambition and avarice—and the designs of the social class that stood behind him—goaded him on to wartime intrigues that eventually saw France fall under humiliating foreign occupation and the restoration of the Bourbon monarchy!

22 June

7 Arab frontline and supporting countries
meet in Tripoli as celebrations of the evacuation
of the US air base conclude.

Abdel Nasser to al-Bakr, the head of the Iraqi
delegation: Unfortunately, we cannot trust you.
Palestine's liberation will be won with blood, not
words. You led the Iraqi delegation that came to
us in 1962 seeking unity between Egypt, Syria and
Iraq—but alas, all your talk turned out to be
lies. You speak of national struggle when you are
really only playing partisan politics.

23 June

Egyptian artillery strikes enemy forces assembled
at al-Shallufa and Port Tawfiq.

Egyptian forces foil enemy attempt to sneak past
Zaafarana.

25 June

Abdel Nasser in Benghazi: We've completed
preparations to cross the canal.

You received a copy of US Secretary of State Rogers' plan while you were in Libya. It proposed a three-month ceasefire and talks between Egypt, Israel and Jordan to negotiate an Israeli withdrawal from the territories occupied in 1967. You thought that this was a lopsided arrangement. It would allow us to fortify our missile batteries and air defence by completing the interception sites that would provide cover for crossing operations to liberate the Sinai. But agreeing to a ceasefire would hurt our soldiers' morale. You put off making a decision about it.

26 June

Egyptian planes attack enemy positions three times.

Air battles over Syria between Syrian and Israeli planes.

27 June

Jordanian Prime Minister Abdel Moneim al-Rifai forms new cabinet.

US announces it will replace planes that Israel lost on the canal front.

28 June

Tel Aviv's foreign minister signs agreement with European Common Market granting Israel preferential tariff treatment with EEC countries.

Nixon orders withdrawal of all forces from Cambodia to bases in South Vietnam.

29 June

Abdel Nasser in Moscow.

US government decides to expedite delivery of
Phantom planes to Israel.

Jordanian army announces dissolution of special
intelligence division at the request of the
Palestinian resistance.

Landowner wanted: Join us and purchase land only.
Build your own apartments to sell and make a
profit of up to 80 per cent in just one year.

Ahmed Kamel, governor of Alexandria, dons sanitation
workers' coveralls to personally oversee campaign
to eradicate flies. Kamel is pictured spraying
pesticides beside the drainage canal.

Dancer Zizi Mustafa tried to enter the Floating
Theatre wearing a dress above her knees. Some of
the audience objected and the situation escalated
to the point where she took off her shoes in
self-defence.

30 June

Beginning of bilateral meetings between Egyptian
delegation led by President Abdel Nasser and
Soviet delegation led by Podgorny.

Egyptian Air Defence downs 4 enemy planes and
takes 3 Israeli pilots hostage.

1 July

Northern Vietnamese government rejects
President Nixon's offer to negotiate until the US
immediately and unconditionally withdraws its
forces from South Vietnam.

3 July

France tests H-bomb in the Pacific Ocean following two other nuclear tests in the Algerian desert two years ago.

Conservative UK government tightens immigration restrictions for coloured settlers from Commonwealth countries.

4 July

President Abdel Nasser was admitted today to the Barvikha sanatorium, located 52 km from Moscow, to undergo medical examinations and a structured treatment regimen on the recommendation of renowned cardiologist Chazov.
Chazov had previously warned Nasser about the risks of working 14 hours per day.

You took the opportunity to discuss the Rogers Plan with the Soviet leadership. You told them that you were leaning towards accepting it for three reasons: First, the scales were shifting in our favour with Israel because of the Soviets' help. Second, we didn't want to provoke a confrontation between them and the US. And third, it would give our forces the opportunity to take a breath and prepare for full-blown military operations. After you announced your acceptance of the plan, the US urged you to ensure a ceasefire would be in place by 8 August.

Egyptian Air Defence downs 2 Israeli Phantom planes.

North Vietnam demands that a date be set for the full withdrawal of US forces before they return to the Paris talks.

Libya nationalizes companies involved in the sale and distribution of petroleum products.

6 July

Two Israeli planes downed and two pilots captured during attack by 16 Israeli planes on the western side of the Suez Canal. Sources in Tel Aviv believe that the Egyptians are already using SA-2 missile defence systems.

US sources indicate that United States intends to establish an air defence umbrella to protect Israel.

Modus vivendi reached between Jordanian government and resistance organizations, ensuring that fedayeen can operate freely.

64,000 stovetops, 12,000 water heaters, 6,500 fridges, 16,000 washing machines, 76,000 televisions, 65,000 radios, 65,000 transistor radios, 41 million dry cell batteries and 20,000 electrical meters slated for production.

7 July

Haim Bar-Lev, IDF chief of general staff, states at a press conference: Egypt has succeeded in installing a new surface-to-air missile system on the Suez Canal front. Soviet experts have been involved in overseeing and launching this system,

which indicates that the Soviet Union has become
directly involved in the conflict.

United Press reports that this past week was the
one of the darkest for the Israeli Air Force:
Israeli planes were downed on the canal front and
five pilots were taken prisoner.

British foreign secretary announces that the UK is
considering resuming arms sales to the apartheid
regime in South Africa.

8 July

Abdel Nasser to remain in Moscow for
ten more days.

Dr Chazov went to Brezhnev and asked him to urge you to stay
for a month of treatment in Moscow. After seeing the test
results, you agreed to stay for two weeks, but you said you'd have
to go back for the Socialist Union's National Congress and that
you needed to be in Egypt before 20 July.

9 July

Resistance destroys Israeli positions in the
Galilee and Jordan Valley.
Another Skyhawk hit during an enemy airstrike at
the front.

50,000 graduates appointed to posts during the new
fiscal year.

Wholesale matchstick industry halted and factory
output turned over to the Food Commodities
Authority so that inventory can be distributed to

retailers via 1,200 branches, finally putting an
end to the crisis.

US sends Israel 6 Phantom planes to replace those
recently lost on the canal front.

Anniversary of the passing of
Lieutenant Mohamed Said Ezzedine.

Tel Aviv attacks UN Secretary General U Thant for
describing Egypt's surface-to-air missile system
as a defensive weapon.

Israeli plane hit and two armoured vehicles
destroyed on the canal front.

The Class of 1969 will start receiving job
appointments this month.

21 merchants arrested after falsely
advertising prices for items on sale.

Gaddafi: Through the Libyan revolution, the people
will own their land.

10 July

Agreement between Jordanian authorities and
resistance leaders on framework for reconciliation
between the two sides.

24 planes clash in heated air battle over the
canal; 2 enemy planes hit.

11 July

Third meeting between Abdel Nasser and
Soviet leaders in the Kremlin lasts
three and a half hours.

Two explosions amid thousands of Israeli
holidaymakers at a summer resort.

12 July

Two groups of Egyptian special forces cross canal
and attack enemy positions.

Missile attacks from the Arab Sinai Organization
strike dozens of enemy targets.

Efforts underway to settle disputes between
resistance and Lebanese government.

Dr Wadie Haddad's home in Beirut bombed at dawn
using timed rockets fired from a fixed base in a
fifth-floor apartment across the street. Haddad is
a Palestinian doctor, resistance leader, and second
in command after George Habash in the Popular
Front for the Liberation of Palestine. The doctor
and members of his family were injured, but
activist Leila Khaled, who was also in the
apartment, was unharmed.

Israel receives 130 cutting-edge radar jamming
devices only two days after requesting the
equipment.

Egyptian forces cross the canal and overwhelm
enemy targets with explosives and machine guns.

Fire breaks out in resistance magazine's
headquarters in London.

PFLP leader killed in battle north of al-Khalil.

14 July

Fierce pressure campaign against Egypt.

Washington hints it is giving Israel arms to prevent it from using nuclear weapons.

Egyptian forces fight back against 56 aircraft striking Egyptian targets.

General Egyptian Organization for Pharmaceuticals recommends that you verify that the cook or worker who prepares your food has a health certificate confirming they do not have any contagious diseases.

15 July

US media creates uproar about Egypt receiving amphibious equipment from the Soviets for crossing the canal.

Israeli authorities impose a curfew on occupied al-Arish after blast targets Israeli military vehicle carrying soldiers.

Third anniversary of the passing of Captain Tawfiq Ahmed Youssef.
Third anniversary of the passing of First Lieutenant Mohamed Maher.

Surprise attack by Arab Sinai Organization destroys enemy communications lines in al-Qantara.

Cable arrives from the Central Committee of the Socialist Union sending greetings and support to President Abdel Nasser.

Now in stores:
Another historical swashbuckler from
Rafael Sabatini—adventure and intrigue at
the French court.

Urban growth swallows up half a million feddans of
agricultural land with another half million
on the way.

16 July

President Abdel Nasser receives a magnificent
welcome at the Supreme Soviet.

Integrated factories in Egypt, India and
Yugoslavia produce subsidized cars to be sold for
700 LE, as well as tractors, scooters and
electronic control modules.

Egyptian Air Defence clashes with Israeli planes.

17 July

New Iraqi constitution safeguards Kurdish rights
and makes Kurdish an official language alongside
Arabic in the Kurdish Region.

Jordanian army withdraws from outskirts of Amman.

New book released in Tripoli: *New Perspectives on
the Market, Mobilization, and Principles of War* by
Colonel Gaddafi, who started writing the book
while he was a lieutenant in the army.

55-year-old dairy merchant kills his 18-year-old
niece and her 25-year-old male friend and cuts
their bodies into small pieces after catching them
in a disgraceful act in her home. He then sat

beside the corpses, smoking and drinking tea until he was arrested.

Miss Alexandria: I will not accept a husband who is much older than me nor a university student who makes only 20 LE per month.

Maxi-swimsuits for summer 1970: cotton, bright colours.
Helanca nylon bathing suits: solid or with geometric designs.

Minister of youth announces that every university student must teach at least ten illiterate people to read. This will make it possible to eliminate illiteracy, which is currently at 70 per cent, within the next five years.

18 July

US Embassy in Tel Aviv: The US Air Force is responsible for protecting Israel.

Egyptian Air Defence downs Israeli Phantom plane and captures a pilot with US nationality.

After two years, al-Azhar allows the play *Husayn the Martyr* by Abdel Rahman al-Sharqawi to be performed, provided that Husayn, Sayeda Zainab and Sayeda Sakina do not appear as characters on stage.

75 years ago in Egypt:
We obtained a copy of the precious treatise written by the Honourable Fathi Zaghoul Bey, head of the court of first instance in Mansoura, entitled *Forgery of Documents*, which he dedicated to his brother, the Honourable Saad Zaghloul Bey,

a judge in the civil court of appeals. The writing is of the highest calibre; we congratulate the esteemed author and encourage everyone to read it.

19 July

1.5 million LE paid in leave allowances to top officials.

Egyptian doctor becomes first microsurgeon in West Germany.

IDF Chief of General Staff expects Egyptians to launch extensive Suez Canal crossing operations soon and stated that Israel is launching intensive airstrikes on the canal front to target Egypt's anti-aircraft batteries.

Egyptian trainer aircraft crashes.
3 pilots killed.

20 July

Israeli Skyhawk plane downed.

US expedites contracts to supply Israeli Air Force with planes and ammunition.

Egyptian Air Defence thwarts enemy's new tack in airstrikes.

21 July

Israeli Skyhawk downed and another hit on the Egyptian front.

Egyptian Foreign Minister Mahmoud Riad in response to US Secretary of State Rogers' plan: Egypt will accept a 90-day ceasefire, during which negotiations would resume to implement UN Resolution No. 242 of 1967, provided that Israel agrees to withdraw from all territories occupied in 1967 and to recognize the Palestinian people's rights.

Libyan Revolutionary Command Council decides to reclaim assets of all 575 Italians in Libya.

All major work on the Aswan High Dam and power plant concluded today.

Time bomb explodes at the palace of Sheikh Khalid bin Mohammed Al Qasimi, ruler of Sharjah.

22 July

Six members of the Palestinian Popular Struggle Front, including one woman, hijack a Greek Boeing 727 after it took off from the Beirut airport. The fedayeen demanded the release of 7 resistance fighters imprisoned in Greece, and the Greek authorities conceded to the hijackers' demands after 7 hours of negotiations. The plane landed at the Cairo airport.

Libyan revolutionary government issues law seizing assets of 620 Jewish persons in Libya and compensates them with nominal state bonds.

Third British military base under construction in Cyprus for British forces withdrawn from Libya.

Luck had been on your side most of the time since the beginning, despite your miscalculations. On that day in 1952 you held a final meeting with the Free Officers at Khaled Mohieddin's home at noon and went over the plan for the coup that would be carried out at 1 a.m. You had decided together that Anwar Sadat would be responsible for cutting off all communications. That evening you drove your Austin to Sadat's house but didn't find him there. The bawab told you that he'd gone with his wife and daughter to the cinema, so then you went to Tharwat Okasha's house where some of the officers were meeting. One of them raised the need for machine guns and you went to see another officer who was in charge of the weapons cache; he wasn't in his apartment either and the lights were off. You set off for another officer's house but a traffic cop on a motorcycle stopped you because your car didn't have rear lights. You continued on to visit other officers and at last went home to al-Galaly Street in Abbasiya. It was a third-floor apartment with four rooms. You took a bath and exchanged a few words with your brothers al-Laithy and Shawky and then kissed your children goodnight: Hoda, Mona, Khalid and Abdel Hamid. Hoda was the oldest—she was six.

You started to get dressed. At 11.05 p.m. one of the officers you knew in the intelligence agency came to inform you that the king had found out about the coup and had called the army's chief of staff. Anyone in their right mind would have called the whole thing off, but you stubbornly insisted on carrying on with the plan. You gave your brothers 100 LE, which was half of what you had with you, and asked them to give the money to your wife if anything happened to you. It was now 11.42 p.m. and Sadat was nowhere to be seen. Amer suggested going to the barracks to see if some of the soldiers would join, but the barracks were closed and there was an unusual number of military police outside so you got out of there quickly. It was now midnight and you both were still driving around unsure of what to do and on the verge of giving up. Suddenly you saw the lights of fifty cars coming from near the Huckstep barracks—it was a platoon from an artillery battalion. They stopped you and one of the young officers announced that he had orders to detain anyone of the rank of lieutenant colonel or higher. You were arrested but fortunately the leader of the battalion was a Free Officer—Lieutenant Colonel Youssef Seddik, a communist. He was on his way to capture the army's general command headquarters in Kobri al-Qubba, an hour before the set time. He let you both go and everyone set off for Kobri al-Qubba where you took control of the building and arrested twenty major generals. Finally Sadat showed up. By 1.30 a.m. you were sitting behind the desk of the army's chief of the general staff.

23 July

President Abdel Nasser announces the completion of the Aswan High Dam power station at the opening of the Fourth National Congress of the Socialist Union on the eighteenth anniversary of the revolution. The president said: We have agreed to the Rogers Plan and will proceed as we see fit in our political endeavours because we are certain that what has been taken by force can't be reclaimed in any other way.

Your wish came true . . . You'd been afraid of dying before the work on the High Dam was complete. It meant a lot to you. It meant everything—it was the culmination of a long struggle and many difficult battles. Now the future would be bright, illuminated by the lamps lit in every village and the factories humming in every city.

Saudi Arabia recognizes the Yemen Arab Republic.

Southern Vietnamese revolutionaries storm base of the US 101st Airborne Division on the outskirts of Huế.
1,700 American casualties and 97 US planes destroyed.

Egyptian Products Sales Co. and its branches in Cairo and the governorates offer an astounding assortment of clothes, radios, TVs and refrigerators.

Dupont lighters:
in duty-free stores for Egyptians, diplomats and foreigners.

In airports:
Skrip
the world's finest ink
packaged at Egyptian Distribution Company facilities under the aegis of Sheaffer, an international company.

24 July

President Abdel Nasser announces to members of the National Congress: We will not hand over the captured Phantom pilots to Israel. The US might be able to replace the Phantom planes but it will be hard to do the same with the pilots.

First anniversary of the passing of Captain Gamil Khalil Abdel Magid.

The secondary-school exam results were in. Your youngest son, Abdel Hakim, passed his exams and would move up from year two to year three. Before the exam, you'd promised him that if he got at least 80 per cent he could ask you for anything and Mohamed Ahmed, your private secretary, would bring it to him right away. Sure enough, Abdel Hakim scored 84 per cent and came to tell you the news. When you congratulated him and asked him what he wanted, he said he'd like to go to London. You said to him, 'Your brothers are taking the gruelling heat on the frontlines and you want to go to London! Once we drive out the Israelis, I'll send you to Tokyo or wherever you like.' Abdel Hakim was fifteen years old and listened to you so he asked the secretary to buy him a motorcycle instead.

25 July

Air Defence fights off 46 Israeli planes.

26 July

That was your day of true glory back in 1956. Your photo appeared on the front page of newspapers around the world, for you had shaken the foundations of the empire on which the sun never sets. It was the day you announced the nationalization of the Suez Canal. Egypt had lost 120,000 men digging the canal, but only saw 1 million out of the 35 million LE that the canal brought in. You stunned the world with a gamble that you miraculously got away with. You weren't expecting war, but it came, testing your men's mettle and your own. Salah Salem broke down and asked you to turn yourself in to the British embassy and Amer wasn't at his best. Even you cried, but on the outside maintained that exceptional fortitude and composure.

At the height of the hostilities, as you stood on the roof of the house with your father, watching the British shelling, you thought of going back to underground work and leading a secret resistance. You were walking on air when you declared at al-Azhar: 'We will fight. We will fight.' You'd insisted on going there alone without any of your colleagues from the Revolutionary Command Council. You imagined vainly that you were the first Egyptian leader to achieve this feat since Ahmose, conqueror of the Hyksos. Being among the masses revived you and you went home high on their chants, your suit torn and your palms scratched by the fingernails of all the people jostling to shake your hand.

Official Egyptian sources announce that Egypt's acceptance of the Rogers Plan does not constitute a new stance vis-a-vis the Palestinian resistance.

Castro offers to resign due to the enormous difficulties that the Cuban economy is facing.

Eighteenth anniversary of the July Revolution.

Grand Cairo soiree at the Qasr El Nil Theatre: Abdel Halim Hafez, Maha Sabry, Nagwa Fouad, Soheir Zaki and Shafik Galal.
Tomorrow at the Qasr El Nil Theatre: *Where It's At,* starring David Janssen.

Sigal Egyptian Company for Metals Trading now offering metal chairs.

First anniversary of the passing of Captain Ahmed Samir Omar.

27 July

Resistance forces reject the Rogers Plan.

Heavy ground fire against 28 Israeli planes.

Meeting of the Preparatory Committee for the
summit of the Non-Aligned Movement.

British lead palace coup in the Sultanate of Oman
to remove Sultan Said bin Taimur and install his
son Qaboos in his place.

Omar Effendi Stores: The big annual sale.

Workers at al-Ahram Beverages:
Increased production is evidence of our pursuit of
victory and our commitment to the principles of
the eternal July Revolution.

Metro Cinema presents: the timeless masterpiece
Gone with the Wind—a stunning success for the
third week straight.

28 July

Our planes attack enemy positions twice and down
one Mirage plane in air skirmish.

Guevara's severed hands and death mask sent to
Cuba after he was killed in the Bolivian jungle.
US intelligence forces cut off his fingers after
he was murdered in 1967.

Authorities find 8 tonnes of drugs smuggled
through Israel in a 6-month period.

Second Asian Student Conference in Hong Kong
refuses to include Israel.

Senate subcommittee discovers that US has had a
base in Morocco since 1963.

29 July

Egypt temporarily bars Palestinian broadcasting
in Cairo due to the stance of certain Palestinian
organizations on Egypt's acceptance of
the US plan.

Ceylon severs diplomatic ties with Israel.

Life sentence for anyone who throws eggs at Milton
Obote, president of Uganda.

British press: British advisors to the Sultan of
Oman led the coup against him.

World Bank raises interest on its loans to
developing countries from 7 to 7.25 per cent.

A newspaper ad for North Korea caught your attention. It was
entitled 'Wars of Liberation' and depicted Kim Il Sung ('the
rising sun') standing in front of a group of soldiers with a large
map of the country behind him. His left hand was on his hip
like in an old European or American oil painting and the caption read: 'Kim Il Sung leads the war of liberation.' Could that
happen to you? That kind of personality cult, almost comical?
You had to admit that many forces seemed to be pushing you
in that direction.

30 July

Menachem Begin: The Rogers Plan is an attempt to
wipe out Israel.

172

Air battle over Ain Sokhna on the Red Sea coast
between 30 planes from both sides. Enemy planes
forced to fall back.

Central Bank of Egypt receives an instalment of
Arab aid worth 6,087,000 LE from Libya.

Egyptian Salt and Soda Company now produces
one-fourth of Egypt's soap and half of its edible
oils.

West Nubariya mechanized farm established in
cooperation with Soviet experts.

31 July

Tel Aviv announces it will accept US plan in
a statement full of ambiguity.
The statement reflects Israel's interpretation of
UN Security Council Resolution 242 on the
withdrawal of forces.

President Nixon: The US is committed to maintaining
the balance of power in the Middle East.

Resistance groups organize silent demonstration in
Amman against the Rogers Plan.

Opening today:
National Folkloric Dance Troupe at
the Balloon Theatre.

1 August

Arab revolutionary forces roundly criticize Abdel
Nasser's acceptance of the Rogers Plan.

Some of the resistance protests were led by a donkey bearing your name. Didn't those stupid revolutionaries realize that the Rogers Plan was going to allow us to catch our breath and prepare for the battle to come—and to set up the anti-aircraft missile system from the Soviets?

92,583 male and female students receive their Egyptian thanawiyya amma diplomas, including 64,315 in the sciences.

Société des auteurs, compositeurs et éditeurs de musique in Paris sends 21,000 LE to Cairo's performing rights association for Egyptian authors and composers (SACERAU) for the broadcasting of their songs and music last year. The largest sum a composer in the association received was 2,600 LE, for the musician Mohammed Abdel Wahab.

2 August

Open letter from Abdel Nasser to the Iraqi government: Wars and liberation struggles are not won with slogans. Why don't you direct your fire at the enemy, and why isn't the enemy firing at you?

Fifth week of the blockbuster film
The Sicilian Clan.

Iraq and Algeria decline to attend the Conference of Frontline Countries in Libya.

Egyptian Air Defence downs Israeli Skyhawk plane in the central sector of the canal.

Salim Rubai, chairman of the Presidential Council
of the People's Republic of South Yemen, visits
China.

Passenger hijacks a Boeing 747, the world's
largest plane, carrying 379 passengers from New
York, and changes its course to Cuba, where he
disembarks. The flight continued on to Puerto
Rico.

3 August

Egyptian Air Defence downs Israeli Phantom plane
over Ismailia and takes its pilot hostage.

Palestinian resistance attacks Israeli factory in
the Upper Galilee.

Egyptian Company for Metals Trading presents
the Nefertiti sewing machine.

24,000 people visit Helwan's sulphur baths
this year.

4 August

Iraqi Revolutionary Court issues new orders for
executions.

Portuguese colonial authorities in Mozambique
dispose of political prisoners by throwing them
out of planes to the lions.

6 August

US forces to invade Laos after Cambodia.

Orabi artist agency presents Nagat el-Sagheera at
Qasr El Nil Cinema.

New branch of Banque du Caire to serve
holidaymakers and residents in the Maamoura area
of Alexandria.

7 August

General Command of the Popular Front for the
Liberation of Palestine backs Egypt's stance.

Skyhawk downed over the city of Ismailia.

Air Defence repels a series of enemy airstrikes
involving 60 planes, resulting in 5 Egyptian
casualties. This occurred an hour before the
ceasefire went into effect as per the US plan.

President Gamal Abdel Nasser:
When I accepted the UN Security Council resolution
in 1967, some friends in the Syrian government
said to me: 'How can you accept this decision? It
will clearly hurt your popularity.' I replied:
'What kind of popularity is bought with empty
words, while those living under enemy control in
Gaza and the West Bank pay the price?' When I
accepted the recent US proposals, which only ask
us to implement the Security Council resolution, I
knew that some groups in the Arab world were going
to yell and scream. But the US did not make these
proposals because of that resolution. There was
something more at play here, forcing their hand
—that the Soviet Union has stood with us and our
fighting capabilities have grown. I accepted the
Rogers Plan to maintain military and international
pressure on the enemy, knowing full well that

these proposals weren't likely to come to anything. We alone are fighting. An official delegation from an Arab country recently went to visit the Soviet Union. During the negotiations, the Soviets put a reference to the November 1967 Security Council resolution in its draft for the joint statement. The head of the Arab delegation said: 'We can't sign a statement that includes that resolution.' The Soviets asked: 'Why?' The head of the delegation said: 'Because we're set on war. There has to be war, and there has to be liberation from the river to the sea.' The Soviets replied: 'But all you want is ten planes and fifty tanks. How can you go to war?' The leader of the delegation said in surprise: 'Who said we're going to fight? Egypt's going to battle, not us!'

Diabetic patients screened and medication distributed.

Men's swimsuits: 7–80 piasters.
Women's swimsuits: 20–170 piasters.

Four Arabic book fairs organized by the Egyptian General Authority for Writing and Publishing in Libya, Sudan and Algeria.

Corona chocolates produced by Alexandria Confectionary & Chocolate Company.

8 August

90-day ceasefire begins on the Egyptian front.

Abdel Nasser receives the commander of the Soviet Air Force.

US Congress discovers that the pharmaceutical industry sold medications to developing countries at many times their actual price.

US Army ignores protests against dumping lethal nerve gas at sea.

US bases accord links Spain with NATO.

Stand-up comedy trio Tholathy Adwa'a El Masrah presents *You've Killed Elaiwa* starring George Sidhom and Samir Ghanem, among others.

Exhaust from 100,000 cars driven in Cairo every day brings air pollution to dire levels.

Zamalek and Ismaily tie 1-1 in an unfortunate match. A pall fell over the game and ruined it.

9 August

Supreme Soviet agrees to build a phosphate and an aluminium factory in the UAR.

Grand summer soiree at Arizona Casino with Abdel Halim Hafez.

New L'Oréal soaps available from Cairo Oils and Soaps Company.

Misr al-Gadida School: a top-tier private school. Al-Ahram Private School: high-quality education.

Poet Salah Abdel Sabour's play
The Princess is Waiting
now showing at the Pocket Theatre.

10 August

Israel engages in double-dealing in its withdrawal
from the occupied territories.

Israel receives 15-million-dollar loan from South
Africa's apartheid government.

Pyjama sets from the Misr Spinning and Weaving
Company in al-Mahalla al-Kubra.

New aluminium plant underway;
will create 3,000 jobs.

Magic eye door viewers now available for 100
piasters from the Egyptian Company for Metals
Trading.

30 plays by 10 playwrights
to be staged next winter, directed by Nabil
al-Alfi, Hamdy Gheith, Saad Ardash, Galal
al-Sharkawy, Karam Mattawa, Abdel Rahim
al-Zarkany, Mahmoud al-Sabaa, Kamal Hussain, Ahmed
Abdel Halim, Ahmed Zaki, Fattouh Nashati, Hassan
Abdelsalam, Hussein Gomaa and al-Sayed Rady, with
plays written by Tawfiq al-Hakim, No'man Ashour,
Abdel Rahman al-Sharqawi, Yusuf Idris, Rashad
Rushdi, Saad Eddin Wahba, Alfred Farag, Ali
Bakathir, Salah Abdel Sabour and Mu'in Bseiso.

Attention ladies: Gas stovetops have become a
household necessity.
Courtesy of the Cooperative Petroleum Company.

Gone with the Wind:
A stunning success for
the fifth week straight.

Abdel Nasser likely to attend the summit of the
Non-Aligned Movement in Zambia on 8 September.

Algerian government asks to withdraw its 2,000
soldiers from the Egyptian front. The soldiers had
arrived in Egypt in June 1967 and the Egyptian
government immediately agreed to the request.

It wasn't a huge loss. You had around 1,700 Algerian, 600
Kuwaiti and 600 Sudanese soldiers. Egypt had to feed, house
and take care of them. Those soldiers cost more than a million
pounds a month! And the building of bunkers, the repairs and
maintenance—all those operations fell on the Egyptian army.
Every six months they sent two battalions of untrained soldiers,
which the Egyptians had to train. As soon as the six months of
training were over, the soldiers would leave and two new battalions would take their place. The same nonsense time and time
again, but what could you do about it?

Israeli press: Egypt began to transport
large-scale military equipment to the Suez Canal
area the same night that the ceasefire went
into effect.

Israeli Foreign Minister: Israel has no 'former
borders'.

Weizman: The Golan Heights and Jordan Valley are
Israel's eastern borders.

6 killed in clashes between resistance groups.

The FBI, led by J. Edgar Hoover, blackmails its enemies by threatening to expose their private lives.

Cambodian revolutionaries now only 7 kilometres from the capital.

Suitcase smuggling under siege:
500 bags containing TVs and fans seized.

200 apartments in Nasr City ready for sale.
Displaced persons from the canal cities offered rent-to-own arrangements.

Names of persons responsible for forming citizens' war committees announced.

The biggest night of the season at Ramses Casino with Fahd Ballan, the voice of the mountain.

Chem
the best detergent
from Kafr al-Zayat Cotton Company.

Air conditioner installed in the ballrooms of the Semiramis Hotel.

12 August

Yasser Arafat makes a surprise visit to Syria and meets with President Nureddin al-Atassi, Prime Minister Yusuf Zuayyin and Minister of Defence Hafez al-Assad.

Fatah's newspaper accuses Mohamed Hassanein Heikal of trying to outdo Israel in bowing to US interests to avoid its ire.

Albanian Prime Minister to Fatah delegation:
The Rogers solution will be at your expense. You
are threatened with death. Albania stands with you
and we are not the only ones. You also have the
support of China, the global centre of liberation
movements.

The following organizations met in the
headquarters of the Palestinian armed struggle in
al-Bawadi camp: The Palestinian National Liberation
Movement (Fatah), the Democratic Popular Front,
al-Sa'iqa (the Lightning Forces), the Popular
Front for the Liberation of Palestine, the Popular
Front for the Liberation of Palestine—
General Command, the Popular Liberation Forces,
the Arab Liberation Front, the Arab Palestine
Organization and the Action Organization for the
Liberation of Palestine.
The groups met to investigate the attack on the
Arab Palestine Organization's office and found
that neither the Popular Front for the Liberation
of Palestine nor any of the other groups had been
responsible.

You knew that most of the groups were affiliated with different
Arab regimes. Each state had its own Palestinian organization.
It was the same as with the Lebanese newspapers.

13 August

He was the first to join the Free Officers. You used to say,
'Amer's my better half, and I'm his.' In the beginning you had
the same way of thinking—complete trust, shared instincts.
Whenever you had a bite to eat or bought new clothing, you'd

send it to Amer too, and he did the same for you. In the beginning, Amer would always tell people in his circles that Abdel Nasser was one in a million and that no one like him would ever exist again, no matter how many children Egypt bore. Amer too was remarkable in his own way. He was smart, affable, never condescending. He made everyone around him love him. He was a proper gentleman from a landowning family. He'd been with you through the siege of al-Faluja and in Sudan. You left him in charge of the armed forces after the revolution but he came up short during the Tripartite Aggression. When you tried to make the necessary changes in the military leadership, he stood by them with the magnanimity of a Saidi mayor and by Sedky Mahmoud, who had demonstrated his own limitations in 1956 and 1967. Amer threatened to resign and you relented. It was the same after the split with Syria, which happened under his office's leadership, and he came back defeated. You forgave him more than once but you began to notice he was changing. He'd started to care about his appearance, about how he dressed—you'd heard about the Berlenti Abdel Hamid saga. Then came the hideous defeat and his collapse.

After you decided not to step down, you put the armed forces directly under your own command and began the process of restructuring the military leadership. That was how you got rid of the problem of Amer, or so you thought. In fact, his house in Giza became a meeting place for several decommissioned officers who were wanted by the authorities. This began to affect order and discipline in the armed forces. There were even some who were under the delusion that the field marshal would return again to lead the army.

You decided to go visit Amer yourself, even though that was a little risky given the officers with weapons holed up there. You called him to let him know that you were coming to see him at home.

Heikal came with you. You tried to make Amer see the consequences of what they were doing. Amer said that the phones were tapped and the police were always around the house, that there were cars watching who came in and went out. He complained that they were targeting the people working with him and you replied that you were ready to look into any matters that were bothering the field marshal but demanded that the people sheltering in his house return to their own homes. Amer became upset and informed you that this was an affront to his manhood. After a quarter hour you and Heikal left, realizing the visit had not been a good idea.

A secret plan was put in place with your approval. Sami Sharaf was in charge of the operation along with Shaarawi Gomaa and Amin Howeidi. The plan involved intercepting the field marshal on the deserted Salah Salem Road as he returned home to Giza in the evening from his headquarters in the military barracks in Helmiyya. He would be held in custody elsewhere, while these locations were brought under control.

On 5 August, Zakaria Mohieddin summoned those three individually to his house at 8 p.m. and they all came together in a show of solidarity. This was not lost on the veteran intelligence man, who told them you'd briefed him on the plan and asked him to go over it with them to see that it was carried out.

There were some changes made to the plan.

On 19 August you received a report from the military intelligence that some officers close to Amer had devised a scheme for him to go to the front where he would announce that he was resuming command of the armed forces. He would then negotiate with you from a position of power to 'get what he was due'. Shams Badran, who was staying at the field marshal's house, had told him that you'd agree to his conditions in order to avoid bloodshed or scandal and suggested that this take place while you were in Khartoum.

On 24 August, you invited all the remaining members of the Revolutionary Command Council—Zakaria Mohieddin, Anwar Sadat and Hussein al-Shafei—to a meeting and explained to them what was happening. Even now, you adhered to the council's hierarchy and seniority system. Everyone agreed that the situation with Amer had become a threat to the security of the army and the country.

You called Amer and invited him to dinner at your house the following day. Perhaps he and those close to him thought you wanted to make a deal. The field marshal came, accompanied by four former Thunderbolt Force officers who served as his bodyguards.

Before he arrived, the men involved in the plan gathered in Sami Sharaf's office and summoned Major General Hassan Talaat, head of the general investigations directorate; then-Major General Mohamed Sadek, the director of military intelligence; Brigadier General Saad Zaglul, the chief of the military police; and Leithy Nassif, the head of the republican guard. Sami Sharaf was ready to record everything that would happen.

When Amer came into the drawing room, he found you with Zakaria Mohieddin, Anwar Sadat and Hussein al-Shafei and looked surprised. Amer said, attempting a smile, 'Is this a trial or what?'

None of you smiled back. You asked him to sit down and then began to speak to him about his behaviour and accused him of conspiring against the regime. He cut you off and said, 'I am involved in no such conspiracy. I deny your claims.'

You replied, 'Amer, you are very clearly conspiring. Let me tell you about one incident I know to be true. You sent your secretary Mahmoud Tantawy to Lieutenant General Sedky Mahmoud five days ago with a message stating that you were planning to seize power and asking him to join you, but Sedky did not agree to this and his wife hurled insults at your secretary and threw him out of the house.'

Meanwhile, Colonel General Mohamed Fawzi and Lieutenant General Abdel Moneim Riad had arrived along with a number of armoured vehicles at Amer's house in Giza. Fawzi sent one of his officers inside the field marshal's house. The officer demanded that everyone surrender their weapons in the name of military order and national duty, and to ensure the safety of the field marshal's family, who were living in the house.

After a few very tense minutes, a fire appeared to have broken out within the house. It turned out that was because Abbas Radwan and Shams Badran were trying to burn various documents and maps in the basement. Then the armoured vehicles assumed an offensive position and everyone inside surrendered. Fawzi and Riad went in to make sure all the weapons were deposited in the basement and that the sixty-one militants inside the house surrendered. They had five anti-tank RPGs, ten boxes of explosive and incendiary hand grenades and twenty-seven boxes of ammunition.

Back at your house, Amer listened to the facts you had just laid out and then stood up, saying that if he had known it was going to be like this he wouldn't have come. He announced that he was going home. He walked to the door of the drawing room and opened it to find a group of armed officers guarding the doorway. He stepped back and said, 'Really? You're going to kill me, then?'

You stood up and said you'd decided he would be put under house arrest at home, and that his house had just been scoured and was now cleared of all the armed men who had been lurking.

Amer collapsed into a chair just as you left the hall. The scene was more than you could bear. He began to yell and then to cry and tried to call for his guards but no one answered because they had already been taken into custody.

When Amer realized that it was no use, he began to surrender. Zakaria Mohieddin spoke to him calmly about the consequences of his actions, and he looked like he was listening. The conversation lasted for more than an hour and then he asked to go to the bathroom. Anwar Sadat went with him and when they returned, Amer announced, 'Tell President Gamal that I've solved the Amer problem for him.' Then he surprised everyone by saying that he'd swallowed poison and was going to die in a matter of minutes and sank into one of the chairs. Immediately the men tried to save him. You heard the commotion from upstairs and came down in a rush. Several hours later the doctors confirmed that Amer was fine. They said that he'd probably claimed to have taken poison just to get a reaction. He was taken

to the Mariotia residence and placed incommunicado except for
a single line. You then took control of the general intelligence
directorate which had been led by Salah Nasr, who was sick at
home.

Several days later your plane took off for Khartoum.

14 August

Al-Minya governorate council bans
the play *Kafr Ayoub*.

Before Mustafa Mahmoud, the devout believer Dr Abd
al-Razzaq Nawfal wrote *God and Modern Science*.
However, Mahmoud takes science as his starting
point, while Dr Nawfal begins with his faith.

In a play performed in Tel Aviv, Israeli generals
declare: 'Our youth are returning from the Suez—
but with only one leg, one arm or one eye. Still,
what matters most is that Israel survives.'

Contractors threaten itinerant workers to prevent
them from cooperating with the Sharqia governor's
project to regulate employment and provide for
their welfare.

You held a meeting at the Maamoura rest-house in Alexandria
with Shaarawi Gomaa, minister of the interior and the Socialist
Union secretary; Sami Sharaf; Hafez Ismail, the director of general intelligence; Fathi al-Dib, who was in charge of Arab affairs;
and Heikal, the minister of information. After the meeting, you
exclaimed to Shaarawi Gomaa, 'How can the Iraqi Ba'ath party
be recruiting officers from the Egyptian armed forces and our
general intelligence?' Shaarawi said he was surprised by the

question since he had nothing to do with the security of the armed forces and that responsibility for these matters lay in the hands of the military intelligence. You said, 'If the Vanguard Organization was effective, no one, including the Ba'ath party, would be able to penetrate Egypt.'

Shaarawi and Sami Sharaf went to the latter's office in Maamoura, which was half a kilometre away. You kept after them on the phone.

Sami picked up the phone and said, 'Yes?' Usually he said, 'Sir?'

'Are you angry at me or what?' you asked.

Sami said, 'Of course not, sir. Why would I be? Nothing to be angry about. You're the commander. It's your right to get upset and be sharp with us.'

You asked him what they had decided. He said they were going to arrest the officers, one of whom was the husband of Kamal al-Din Refaat's daughter, and you gave your approval for their decision.

15 August

Israel launches attack on Jordanian territory.

Cairo announces that it is not prepared to respond to Israeli allegations regarding an Egyptian anti-aircraft missile battery on the canal front since the ceasefire began.

Israeli forces slip into Lebanon and blow up 3 houses, then return across the border with two Lebanese citizens.

Lebanese Interior Minister Kamal Jumblatt lifts
bans against the Communist Party, the Syrian
Social Nationalist Party and the Arab Socialist
Ba'ath Party.

Golda Meir asks leaders of US Zionist
organizations to raise a billion dollars to
replenish the Israeli economy.

US uses satellites and spy planes in
reconnaissance missions over the canal.

Cambodian coup government issues life sentence to
wife of deposed Prince Sihanouk, the country's
legitimate leader, for allegedly smuggling weapons
to revolutionaries.

Soviet Union launches spacecraft towards Venus
which will arrive by the end of the year.

20 August

King Hussein in Cairo to meet with Abdel Nasser.

Syrian authorities accuse Iraq of attempting to
stage a coup in Syria.

Japanese man hijacks passenger plane using
a toy gun.

22 August

Lebanese schools grant thanawiyya amma diplomas to
Egyptian students with any grade they want.

Investigations launched into clandestine
organization linked to Iraqi Ba'ath Party in Cairo.

The juvenile Left: short-sighted and naive.

Soviet Union tests two new multi-headed
nuclear missiles.

Oversight report: Most artistic works produced by
the General Cinema Foundation are created by
employees of the organization itself, including
Saad el-Din Wahba (who received 12,000 LE between
February and September 1968), Youssef Gohar
(11,000 LE between January 1968 and March 1970),
Abdel Rahman al-Sharqawi (5,000 LE between
December 1967 and June 1969) and Naguib Mahfouz
(5,000 LE between January and December of 1969).

13 killed in train accident in Upper Egypt.

Muharram Fouad sings 'I Want a Girl'
by Abdel Rahman el-Abnudi.

24 August

An Israeli spokesperson said that work on Egyptian
missile bases began on 19 August and that each
base had 6 launch platforms with a reinforced
command system in the middle.

25 August

Sudanese Revolutionary Council issues resolution
to nationalize the press.

Abdel Nasser receives Yasser Arafat and a
delegation from Fatah's central committee twice in
a single day.

The General Assembly of the International Astronomical Union, held in Brighton, announces it has found a new solar system separate from our Earth's solar system.

Matrouh express train crashes near Damanhour.

27 August

US and British press in uproar about the continuous flow of weapons shipments that Egypt has been receiving from the Soviet Union, and which include anti-aircraft missiles, amphibious vehicles and heavy artillery with a 60-km plus range.

Armed clashes erupt between the Palestinian resistance and Jordanian army on a street in Amman, while intense fighting continues between the resistance and Israeli forces on the Jordanian front, during which three resistance officers were killed.

29 August

Jordanian army launches full-blown artillery and tank attacks on Palestinian resistance positions in Amman.

Israel moves towards withdrawing from talks with UN Special Representative Jarring.

31 August

Nixon announces that he will give up on pursuing cooperation with the Soviet Union on joint efforts to preserve peace in the Middle East.

Air Algérie flight hijacked and rerouted to
Dubrovnik Airport in Yugoslavia.

1 September

Nasser arrives in Libya to celebrate the first
anniversary of Gaddafi's coup.

Renewed clashes between the resistance and
Jordanian army.

2 September

US Secretary of Defense announces that the US is
continuing to send Phantom planes to Israel.

3 September

Tel Aviv announces that it will suspend communications with UN Special Representative Jarring.

Institute for Strategic Studies announces that
Egypt has 415 planes while Israel has 330.

Israeli sources state that Israel has lost 13
Phantoms on the canal front.

5 September

30 people killed in heated fighting between
Jordanian army and Palestinian resistance in
Zarqa, 25 km north of Amman.

Libyan government decides to halt aid to Jordan
until the trajectory of the conflict between the
Jordanian army and the resistance becomes clearer.

Israeli minister of defence announces that US must push for removal of Egyptian missiles or Israel will withdraw its support for the ceasefire.

Leftist candidate Salvador Allende declares victory in the Chilean presidential elections.

India's Council of States rejects bill to abolish privy purses and special privileges of maharajas.

6 September

Palestinian fedayeen attempt to hijack 4 planes operating with US, Israeli and Swiss airlines.

Pan American jumbo jet with 177 on board forced to land at the Cairo airport and then blown up by eight time bombs after passengers evacuate.

Israeli plane seized by Palestinian resistance fighter Leila Khaled forced to land in London, where she is detained.

52 dead and 210 wounded after clashes in Jordan between the resistance and the army.

Israel announces it will withdraw from talks with Jarring.

7 September

Switzerland and West Germany announce that they will release Arab fedayeen imprisoned in their countries in exchange for hijacked planes and their passengers, who are held in resistance bases in Jordan.

Bloody clashes in Jordan continue.

8 September

Armed clashes erupt again between the army and resistance in Jordan after a new agreement had been signed to resolve the situation.

Major scandal brews in Lebanon:
Modern prison under construction by French company with initial costs estimated at 6 million Lebanese lira, but 16 million has already been spent on the prison so far. Developers have asked for another 4 million, with 22 million more required to bring the project to completion. The project is under the oversight of Malik Salam, the head of the Executive Council for Major Projects, who is married to the sister of Prime Minister Rashid Karami and is the brother of former Prime Minister Saeb Salam.

Working housewives in Giza have found a solution to time constraints which have sometimes forced them to give their husbands only sardines, bully beef and Roumi cheese for lunch. The Economic Liberation Association has now created a system through which they can request homemade meals by phone, prepared by evacuees from the canal cities.

9 September

Palestinian fedayeen hijack a British passenger plane carrying 128 people on its way from Bombay to London and force it to change course to Revolution Airport in northern Jordan.

US announces new deal to send Israel 45 more Phantom planes.

UAR celebrates Fellahin Day, marking the
anniversary of the first agricultural reform law
after the 1952 Revolution.

10 September

Britain begins to evacuate its nationals from
Jordan as clashes continue.

11 September

Aircraft carrier and naval support units from US
Sixth Fleet reach the eastern Mediterranean near
the coast of occupied Palestine.

Tel Aviv asks US for new arms deal worth
800 million dollars.

During a Cabinet meeting, you said to Dr Aziz Sedky, the minister of industry, 'Dr Aziz, the new school year has begun and the price of locally manufactured clothes is outrageous. People are writing to me, asking, Who could possibly afford a shirt that costs a whole pound? A sweater for 2 pounds? Socks for 25 piasters and overshirts for 50? If you have five children you need 20 pounds just for sweaters and socks for their uniforms. How much must state employees pay to buy clothes, shoes, rulers, erasers and notebooks for their sons and daughters to go to school? If you don't bring these prices down, I'm going to have to import these products from China and let them sell that stuff in Soliman Pasha Square . . .'

12 September

Popular Front for the Liberation of Palestine
blows up 3 hijacked planes because their demands
have not been met.

Ceasefire reinstated in Amman between Jordanian
army and Fatah.

Soviet Union launches a new spacecraft to
the moon.

14 September

New clashes in the city of Irbid.

US Secretary of State Rogers announces to the
Senate that the US Department of Defense will
agree to fund further arms for Israel because
President Nixon believes that it is in
the US interest to arm Israel.

400 homes to be built in new Jewish neighbourhood
in the Arab city of al-Khalil.

Another tragic day for you.

The stage was the Mariotia, and the actor, Abdel Hakim Amer, who was confined there. On the morning of that day in 1967, the field marshal refused to eat anything except for some fluids because he kept vomiting. They gave him medication but he still couldn't keep anything down so he was given a glucose IV and remained under medical supervision. At five o'clock the steward called for help and the doctor came running and found Amer in a coma with a weak pulse. He was given a shot of Coramine and hooked up to artificial ventilation with an oxygen cylinder. They found a band-aid on his body containing the poison aconitine, which if ingested results in death within four hours. At 5.40 p.m. Amer stopped breathing.

15 September

Agreement reached to end Jordanian army's siege of Amman and for withdrawal of resistance forces from their positions in the heart of the capital.
One resistance leader said: We have tried to contact the army's chief of staff, Major General Mashour Haditha, to discuss implementation of the agreement. At 10.30 a.m. we called the Royal Palace and it became apparent that the king had formed a new military ministry. A few hours later the telephone rang in the central committee's headquarters and our brother Yasser Arafat spoke with Brigadier General Mohamed Daoud, head of the new military government in Jordan. Daoud asked for an urgent meeting with members of the central committee to implement the agreement. Arafat told him that forming the new military government violated the agreement and the call ended. We are declaring a general strike starting tomorrow to bring down the military government and restore the national government. We have begun to see columns of armoured vehicles and tanks belonging to the Jordanian army headed in all directions...

You were exhausted. The pain was getting worse and you decided to go to Marsa Matrouh for a full week's rest.

Instead the crisis in Jordan spiralled out of control.

At first, everyone was hesitant to call you while you were away, during those early days of the crisis. But in the evening you heard what had happened on the radio and made calls asking to be told all the details.

Muammar Gaddafi came to Marsa Matrouh the next day and several messages from Yasser Arafat were relayed to you over the phone.

You decided to send Lieutenant General Sadek to Amman with a message for the king. Then Gaddafi and Jaafar Nimeiry attached their names as well.

You followed the developments minute by minute in the train from Cairo to Alexandria with your wife and son Abdel Hakim as well as Hussein al-Shafei and Fawzi, the minister of war. You told them that you hadn't seen your youngest son Abdel Hamid in two months and you were going to miss him again because he was at the naval academy and you had to travel tomorrow to Marsa Matrouh to meet Gaddafi. In the evening, when you'd arrived at your residence in Maamoura in Alexandria, Abdel Hamid called his mother and said that his commander at the academy had told him he had permission to go to the president's residence. He complained that this had embarrassed him in front of his peers and said he didn't want to come right then. Abdel Hamid asked her, 'Did you ask them to let me go?' You took the telephone receiver and said to your son, 'I really miss you, Mido.' You listened to him for a moment and then said, 'Do what you want.' He came home later that day and his mother brought him to your room. You shook his hand and kissed him. 'You smoke!' you remarked, laughing. 'How many cigarettes a day? Don't smoke too much or when you get old the doctors will make you stop.' The boy ate dinner with the whole family and said that he had refused to leave the academy at first. Then the officer on duty told him, 'You must go now—

we have an order.' You asked him, 'When do you have to be back?' Abdel Hamid said, 'Tomorrow at ten in the morning, but I want to go back tonight so I can be with the other students in the morning.' You told him, 'It's up to you.' He went back to the academy after dinner and that was the last time you saw him.

16 September

King Hussein imposes martial law in Jordan and appoints Habis Majali, his military advisor, as commander-in-chief and Major General Zaid ibn Shaker as deputy chief of operations for the army.

344,000 General Motors workers go on strike. Daily losses for the company estimated at around 100 million dollars.

Golda Meir, prime minister of Israel, departs for US visit.

17 September

At dawn on Thursday, heavy fighting began in the streets of Amman. The Jordanian army stormed the capital with its tanks to expel the fedayeen. They fired on anything that moved with mortars, heavy machine guns, armoured vehicles and non-rebounding 6-mm artillery guns. The Jordanian forces surrounded 50 resistance fighters on a street near the US information bureau and killed them. Their bodies were taken to one of the main streets. It was broadcast over the radio that Field Marshal Habis Majali had granted absolute powers to the army to quell the situation. By noon, the fighting extended to several other cities. Field Marshal

Majali, the commander-in-chief, repeated the same orders over the radio, calling on the army to 'cleanse Jordan of fedayeen outposts'. The resistance has more than 120 branches and media offices across various parts of the capital and has set up nests of heavy machine guns on the rooftops of these buildings.

Field Marshal Majali on Radio Amman:
We will rain misery on the hijackers who kidnapped people, who forcibly rerouted planes, took hostages and stormed hotels and schools. Trouble is coming to those who bombed the houses of innocents, cut off their water and obstructed the work of state agencies.

Gaddafi arrives at Marsa Matrouh to meet with Abdel Nasser.

18 September

Fighting spreads to five Jordanian cities. In Amman, battles move from house to house. Casualties have now reached 500.

Lieutenant General Sadek arrives in Amman with a message from Abdel Nasser, Nimeiry and Gaddafi and meets with King Hussein and Yasser Arafat.

Fighting in the streets between the army and the resistance.

Amman cut off from the world: The airport has been shut down, telecommunications are cut off and a total curfew has been imposed on the city.

Thick smoke rises over the city from fires started by artillery shots.

Three messages from Arafat to Abdel Nasser asking
for his immediate intervention to stop the
conspiracy. Arafat accuses the king of having
issued orders to bomb and destroy Amman.

Iraqi forces pull back from the fighting in Jordan
and allow the Jordanian army to take up offensive
positions against the fedayeen.

Shwikar and Fouad el-Mohandes on Channel 5 this
afternoon in the film *Shanabo in the Trap*.

19 September

Arab Liberation Front forces affiliated with the
Iraqi Ba'ath party withdraw from their positions
in Jabal Amman, leaving a perilous gap in the
resistance's defences.

Bombing of refugee camps
on the outskirts of the capital.
Bedouin soldiers wearing green berets loot shops.

At 2.20 p.m. Majali issues a warning
to the fedayeen to surrender by 5 p.m.

20 September

Radio Cairo cuts short its regular programming at
noon and broadcasts an urgent telegram from
President Abdel Nasser to King Hussein.

Abdel Nasser calls for a cessation of hostilities.

President Abdel Nasser to King Hussein: Our
information suggests that the losses are tremendous.
There are thousands of innocents under fire or
bleeding out in the streets.

Abdel Nasser to Yasser Arafat: Egypt is keeping a close eye on the Palestinian resistance, just as we are with the Jordanian army.

Nixon follows developments in Jordan hour by hour with advisors Kissinger and Haldeman from his residence at Camp David.

US actions indicate conflict is escalating in Jordan.

Nimeiry accuses US intelligence of engineering violence in Jordan.

King Hussein issues order to his forces for a ceasefire beginning at 7 p.m.

Thousands lie dead and wounded in the streets of the Jordanian capital Amman.

Residents face grave shortages of food and water.

Jordanian tanks and infantry attack Palestinian Red Crescent Hospital.

Radio of the central committee of the resistance: Amman is burning, Amman is burning.

Radio Amman broadcasts a final warning.

Radio of the central committee of the resistance: The daughter of Brigadier General Daoud, head of the military government in Jordan, makes a radio appeal to her father, asking him to resign and stand in solidarity with the Palestinians.

King Hussein meets with US ambassador in Jordan to discuss developments after previous efforts to meet had failed.

A soft landing for Soviet spacecraft Luna 16 in
Mare Fecunditatis on the surface of the moon,
after a 4.5-day journey from the Earth.

Abdel Nasser calls for an Arab League summit.
Arab heads of state begin to arrive in Cairo.

22 September

Delegation led by Nimeiry flies to Amman in the
afternoon.

Civil war in Jordan enters its sixth day
while Arab League summit is convened in Cairo.

Official Jordanian delegation in Cairo led by
Jordanian Prime Minister Brigadier General
Mohamed Daoud.

US announces it will evacuate its nationals from
Jordan and warns of potential US intervention.

President Abdel Nasser has gone to stay in a
private suite on the thirteenth floor of the Nile
Hilton for the course of the summit proceedings.

24 September

Violent clashes continue in Amman and spread
to Irbid.

Palestinian Red Crescent recommends drinking urine
given the lack of potable water.

British correspondent: Jordanian soldiers have
broken the fingers of all of the men and boys in
houses where they found any remnants of
projectiles.

Nimeiry sends telegram to King Hussein in the name of the Arab leaders gathered in Cairo: If the news is true, this is a violation of what we agreed upon with regard to a full and immediate ceasefire. The king responds that there is no fighting taking place between the two sides. Brigadier General Mohamed Daoud, prime minister of Jordan, submits his resignation to King Hussein from Cairo.

Arab heads of state send a large delegation to Amman from Cairo at 4.40 p.m. and meet with King Hussein immediately after their arrival.

At 11.10 p.m. Radio Amman broadcasts an appeal from President Nimeiry to Mr Yasser Arafat asking how he might best reach him.

Radio Amman repeats the call several times.

At 12.45 a.m. the radio of the central committee in Damascus broadcasts a reply from Yasser Arafat: My brother, President and Major General Jaafar Muhammad Nimeiry—in response to your request, let us meet tonight around 1 a.m. We suggest that you come in your car from the road leading from the Caravan Hotel and Princess Alia School to the Embassy of the United Arab Republic in Jabal al-Weibdeh, from which point we will have a representative accompany you to the meeting place.

Massacre of Palestinians in Irbid.

25 September

Casualties of brutal fighting in the last week surpass 15,000—more than the number of casualties in the 1948 War, the 1956 Tripartite Aggression or June 1967.

Pictured above: A helicopter kept at the ready
atop the roof of King Hussein's palace.

Abdel Nasser receives resistance leaders Salah
Khalaf (Abu Iyad), Farouk al-Kaddoumi (Abu al-Lutf),
Ibrahim Bakr and Bahjat Abu Gharbia at the Cairo
airport after they are freed from detention
in Amman.

Lebanese newspaper reports that the four were
detained together while trying to leave the
central committee headquarters in Jabal
el-Hussein. Their guards were killed and they were
taken to the al-Hummar Palace cellars and the next
day put in a tank that drove them around various
neighbourhoods of Amman so they could see the
dead, the wounded, the hungry, the fires, the
total destruction.

New numbering for 175 bus lines.
Cartoon of a citizen uncertain about which bus
to take. Caption: People are stupid. Right,
because 1 is now 890 and 1 with one stroke is 908
and 1 with two strokes is 890 and 2 with one
stroke is 704 and 3 is 841 and 3 with a stroke is
now 851 and 4 with a stroke is 943. And they say
we don't understand?

Iraqi Vice President: The Iraqi army is staying at
the front and will give anyone working against the
resistance a lesson they will never forget.

26 September

Jordanian artillery strikes Egyptian embassy while
Arab heads of state are still inside.

Arab heads of state broker an agreement between
Yasser Arafat and King Hussein for an immediate
ceasefire.

King Hussein speaks on Radio Amman to give
orders for an immediate ceasefire.
Sudanese president delivers order from Yasser
Arafat, general commander of the Palestinian
revolutionary forces, to cease hostilities.

As the Arab heads of state returned from the
al-Hummar Palace to the Egyptian embassy after
reading their statements over the radio, the
horrific bombings continued. The Ashrafiya
Hospital was bombed and hundreds of children,
women and the infirm were put out in the street
and mechanisms to eliminate them were devised.
Doctors and nurses were kidnapped. All of
this happened while the ink had not even dried on
the ceasefire agreement. When the delegation
reached the Egyptian embassy, heavy fire rained
down on the building. President Nimeiry personally
called King Hussein and informed him of the
gravity of the situation and had him listen to the
sound of gunfire on the phone. The king fell
silent for a moment and then said, 'I'll do what
needs to be done.' He sent Major General Mohamed
Khalil, the deputy chief of staff of the army;
Ahmad Toukan, the chief of the Royal Hashemite
Court; and Zaid ibn Shaker, the deputy chief of
operations, who were not able to enter the embassy
until after they got into an armoured car. Once
inside, they spoke to the military operations
command on the phone and asked them to stop firing
immediately, which they did.

Delegation leaves Amman at 7 p.m. in an armoured car and is fired on by the army.

Yasser Arafat arrives in Cairo at 11.45 p.m. and immediately goes to the Nile Hilton where he meets with the Arab heads of state.

President Nimeiry smuggles Arafat through in his car, disguised in Kuwaiti attire.

You were filled with excitement. The youth could do the impossible—like you had once done. What did the future hold for them: Nimeiry, Gaddafi, Arafat? What would the responsibilities, temptations and perils of power do to them?

US State Department announces that King Hussein has asked the US for large quantities of food supplies and ammunition. Nixon says he will help Jordan restock the equipment and weapons it lost during battles with the resistance and provide a 5-million-dollar grant.

Brigadier General Mohamed Daoud seeks asylum in Libya.

100,000 Jordanians have lost their homes.

Red Cross: What is happening in Jordan defies belief. There are corpses rotting in the streets, thousands of houses destroyed and hundreds of people under the rubble.

Egyptian minister of local administration: The local administration system is following its set course exactly.

Moshe Dayan: Fortunately for Israel, the fighting between the Jordanian army and the resistance is far away from us.

At 4 a.m. an urgent telegram is sent from Abdel Nasser to Hussein:

To His Majesty King Hussein bin Talal: In the name of the Arab heads of state gathered in Cairo, I regret to inform you of our grave concerns after the reports that we have heard from our brother President Jaafar Nimeiry and the other members of our delegation who have returned from Amman. The reports that we have all heard confirm several facts beyond any possible doubt: The Jordanian authorities continue to insist on fighting despite all the efforts that have been made. All promises made to us have become utterly devoid of meaning. There are detailed plans in place to liquidate the Palestinian resistance despite claims to the contrary. The delegation, which has now returned from Amman, felt that they were subject to underhanded dealings to which they should not have been subjected. In light of all of this, we have agreed that President Nimeiry will hold a press conference, during which he will speak on behalf of all the members of the committee that joined him on that mission and relay the particulars of their reports to us. We feel immense sorrow that matters have escalated to this level, but what is happening now leaves no other course of action. The truth must be told and our Arab nation must always rise above evil and emerge stronger than any machinations.

Press conference with President Nimeiry: King
Hussein alone bears full responsibility for
carrying out these criminal plans on behalf of
Israel and the US to slaughter the entire
Palestinian resistance and all Palestinians
living in Jordan.

Hussein sends a telegram to Abdel Nasser expressing
his regrets regarding what was said at the
conference at a time when Jordan is undergoing an
ordeal. Hussein said that the situation in Jordan
required prompt action and due haste in
implementing the recent agreement in both letter
and spirit.

Jordanian forces have detained 14,000
Palestinians.

Hussein forms new government under
the leadership of Ahmad Toukan, the chief of the
Royal Hashemite Court.
Toukan is disowned by his family.

Hussein asks to visit Cairo.

Thick black smoke rises over Palestinian refugee
camp in Jabal Amman.
Libya severs diplomatic ties with Jordan.

Pictured above: Arab heads of state meet at dawn
with Yasser Arafat in the Nile Hilton in Cairo.

The problem was that you were a giant among dwarfs. Couldn't
they see the enemy's plan? Some of were clearly aware but
others looked the other way and with some you really couldn't
be sure. You thought: We'll try to avoid the traps set for us and

most of all, stop the bloodshed. We'll prepare for battles we do not want to fight, battles we'll avoid if we can—but we are ready.

Egyptian doctors invited to volunteer for medical missions to Jordan.

IDF Chief of General Staff: If the situation in Jordan continues, Israel will engage in a military operation of a different scope and nature than any carried out previously.

US Department of Defense spokesperson announces that the Soviet Union has started to build a submarine base in Cuba.

Nixon arrives in Naples to inspect the US Sixth Fleet's most powerful naval vessels: Three aircraft carriers with 300 fighter-bomber planes plus artillery batteries and missile launch bases, preceded by battleships and missile frigates, and then a fleet of torpedo boats and minesweepers. Nixon is expected to watch this exercise, which will begin at 10 p.m. on 28 September, from the bridge of the aircraft carrier, USS *Saratoga*.

New York Times journalist Max Frankel from aboard the USS *Saratoga*: Only one thing can be meant by these exercises—Gamal Abdel Nasser in Cairo will hear the Sixth Fleet's guns.

Nixon arrives in Rome.

Third anniversary of the passing of the martyr Captain Mohamed Mokhtar Zaki Qassim.
Anniversary of the passing of Squadron Leader Nour al-Suweifi.

211

Benha Company for Electronic Industries:
19-inch television that gives you a steady
picture automatically.
Transistor radio that runs on 4 flashlight
batteries.

In celebration of the beginning of the holy month
of Ramadan, the company will waive purchase fees
(valued at 3 LE) for anyone who buys a
Catron television.

US Department of Commerce announces that the net
profit of US companies operating in Latin America
was 2,400 million dollars, over 50 per cent more
than in 1960, when the Alliance for Progress was
unveiled.

Sunday, 27 September

In the afternoon, the Arab League summit held a whirlwind session, which King Hussein attended for the first time. It began around 1 p.m. and the room was tense: King Hussein with some of his officers in a corner, Yasser Arafat at the edge of his seat, barely containing his nerves and King Faisal in his usual chair for these meetings with his hand on his cheek, thinking.

You came in and headed towards where Faisal was sitting. He quickly accosted you, 'Mr President, I do not want to sit among all these guns.' You said, laughing, 'You don't have to, I'll sit among the guns. Go ahead, take my seat.'

The session ended at 3.30 p.m. and then there was a meeting with the heads of state only. You said, 'We understand that King Hussein has come because he wants to find a solution, and that the Palestinian resistance have agreed to have him here because they too want a solution. We must therefore discuss how to put an end to this calamity and to keep these unfortunate events from further escalating.'

When the meeting ended, Heikal was waiting for you in your suite. Half an hour later he left and you went into your bedroom to rest before the evening session, which was supposed to begin at six. Heikal returned at five after changing his shirt and tiptoed into your suite. He found your attendant Mohamed Dawoud standing at the door of your bedroom. Dawoud said to Heikal, 'The president is sleeping and has asked to be woken at 5.30 p.m.'

Several minutes later Mohamed Ahmed, your private secretary, came and said, 'President Nimeiry and Bahi Ladgham are coming now. Should we wake him?'

Heikal looked at his watch. It was only 5.07 p.m. 'Let's wait a little and give him a few more minutes of sleep,' he said. The two went to greet Nimeiry and Bahi Ladgham, and Heikal whispered that the president was sleeping but that they could wake him if they wished.

Nimeiry said, 'Let's leave him a while. We have come about the draft agreement that we need to draw up in light of the discussions from the previous session, and which will be the basis of our discussions in tonight's session.'

They waited all the way until 5.30 p.m. when Mohamed Dawoud called Heikal to the bedroom. Heikal found you standing by the bedside and you said, 'Go join them—I'm going to take a quick bath and I'll be with you shortly.' You added, 'I was in a deep sleep because I was so exhausted.'

At 5.30 p.m. you went to join them in the drawing room. You picked up the draft agreement but couldn't find your glasses so you turned the pages for Heikal and asked him to read it to you. You said that the draft might be an acceptable starting point if 'intentions were good'.

Mohamed Ahmed arrived with a message for Heikal from Yasser Arafat, who was staying on the fourth floor of the hotel. You asked about the contents of the message and Heikal replied, 'Arafat has information from Amman that the Jordanian army is intensifying its attacks to try to take control of Amman tonight. He wants directives for the Egyptian monitoring officers who flew to Amman this morning so they can begin their work.'

'Let's have Yasser Arafat come look at the draft agreement with us before the session. And go ask whether Gaddafi is ready to join us here,' you said.

Arafat arrived in a state of agitation. 'Mr President, how can we trust these people who are set on eradicating us while we are here talking? There's no point. We have to just bring it all crashing down and then see what happens.'

You replied, 'Yasser . . . We can't do anything now that will spin this further out of control. We must constantly ask ourselves: What's the objective? We have agreed that the objective is a ceasefire as quickly as possible. I have set out with this purpose in mind, taking the circumstances into account, as per your request to me at the beginning. Your position in Amman is dire and your men in Irbid are under siege. I have told you from the outset that we can't help through direct military intervention from our side. That would be a misstep—then we'd have to stop fighting Israel to fight in Jordan, which would also open the door to foreign intervention. They're waiting for an opportunity like that. I am trying to win time so that I can bolster your capacity to resist and help you reach a reasonable solution. In the past few days I've opened all the stops for arms and ammunition and I've asked Brezhnev to have the Soviets pressure the US not to intervene. You asked me to do this and I have done it. All this I've done so that we can buy time to prevent a mortal blow against the resistance. With every bone in my body I have worked to protect you. I could have just issued a statement in support and given you a radio station to say whatever you wanted against the king and then sat back to watch. But my conscience did not allow me to do that. I could end the conference right now. From a political standpoint the summit has already achieved a great deal. Nimeiry went to Amman and came back with four resistance leaders whom he got out of prison, and went back again and returned with you. Then Nimeiry and the delegation that went with him made their report, which clarified the facts of the situation and has helped ramp up pressure. I can leave things as they are and rest but instead I must ask myself and ask you: What's our objective? That is the question we cannot lose sight of. Our objective is still a ceasefire, to give you a chance to reassess your position and regroup your forces. We now have the chance to reach an agreement. Are we going to try, or give up now and abandon our objective? It is your decision. From the outset I have been here to support and protect you, to protect the innocent who were killed without anyone to bury them, the wounded who have no one to treat them, the women and children despairing amid the rubble, searching in vain for the most basic of human rights—the right to a secure life.'

You were worked up. Sadat noticed this and offered to make you a cup of coffee. He went into the kitchen in your suite and had Mohamed Dawoud, who was attending to the president, leave. Sadat prepared the coffee himself and handed you the cup. You drank it.

Silence fell. Then Gaddafi arrived and the other heads of state proceeded to the meeting hall so the session could begin. You asked Arafat, 'Shall we go? And are we going to disperse the meeting or continue discussions to reach our objective?'

Nimeiry said, 'Let's go now.'

Everyone took the lift down to the meeting hall on the second floor. Arafat gripped Heikal's hand and leaned towards him, saying, 'Nasser—he was destined to bear the burdens and blunders of all Arab peoples.'

Because this meeting was only for the heads of state, Heikal, who had attended earlier in his capacity as the Egyptian minister of information, went back up to the eleventh floor where Anwar Sadat was staying. Sadat was sitting on the balcony with his radio in front of him, trying to tune it to a particular station. Then Heikal went to his office at al-Ahram and found there was a telephone call from the chief of protocol saying that the president wanted him immediately in the meeting hall. He returned quickly to the Hilton.

You saw Heikal and summoned him to your side, murmuring, 'The agreement's done. They're preparing the final typewritten version now so we can all sign it.'

After a day of concerted work and six days of continuous meetings, the assembled leaders (King Faisal, King Hussein, Gamal Abdel Nasser, Yasser Arafat, Bahi Ladgham of Tunisia, Suleiman Frangieh of Lebanon, and Ahmad al-Shami of Yemen) had reached an agreement between Jordan and the resistance to end military operations. Both sides would withdraw their forces from Amman and restore the situation in northern Jordan as it had been before. The agreement was signed at 9 p.m. on Thursday. During the signing, you stood between King Hussein and Yasser Arafat with his dark glasses and rolled-up sleeves, the Palestinian kufiyya on his head.

You went up to your suite and stood on the balcony looking out over the Nile with Anwar Sadat, Hussein al-Shafei, Ali Sabri and Heikal. You were telling them in your buoyant way about some of what had happened during the meeting when suddenly you looked around and asked, 'Where is Muammar Gaddafi?'

Mohamed Ahmed appeared shortly after with the news that Gaddafi was already on his way from the meeting hall to the airport to return to Benghazi, having shaken hands with President Abdel Nasser earlier.

You immediately said, 'Call the airport and have them hold the plane until I get there. I have to say farewell myself.' Then you added, 'I think that there is no reason now for me to stay in the hotel. I miss the children. Perhaps I can see them before they go to bed.'

Heikal went with you as far as the lift and said goodbye before the door closed. Neither of you knew it would be the last time you would shake hands.

You went to the airport to see off Muammar Gaddafi and then went back to al-Qubba Palace, where you gathered with your small family for the first time in more than a week. At 11 p.m. you went to your bedroom and your youngest son Abdel Hakim came after you, saying, 'I want to go see the Indian film *Boot Polish* at the Odeon or *Sunset and Sunrise* with Soad Hosni at Diana Cinema.' 'Of course, my dear,' you replied.

Then you picked up the telephone receiver and spoke to your aide Sami Sharaf.

'What are we going to do about Khalid's military service when he finishes the academy this year?' you asked.

Sami said, 'Sir, do you have a particular plan in mind or would you like me to consult with Colonel General Fawzi about the matter?'

You said, 'I think he should be in the army and join the Republican Guard as a normal citizen under Leithy's supervision, because I'm concerned that if he's put in any other unit, there would be favouritism and he wouldn't get much out of it. But in the guard with you and Leithy, he'd be like any other soldier—no special treatment or privileges. What do you think? Ask Fawzi anyway, and Leithy. We can talk about it tomorrow. What's the latest news from the front?'

Then you turned off the light in your bedroom.

At 12 a.m. the British ambassador arrived with a telegram detailing the exchange of the seven who had been captured and detained in the UK for the hostages from the plane that had been hijacked to Jordan. The ambassador asked that the telegram be delivered to President Abdel Nasser immediately.

Heikal called Sami Sharaf, minister of state and the president's secretary of information, and asked, 'Is the president asleep? Is the light off in his room?'

Sami replied, 'He was just talking with me now. You can call him quickly.'

Heikal dialled your number and you picked up. He began to apologize for bothering you, but you told him gently, 'Never mind, there's still plenty of time before I go to sleep. I was just thinking about what's happening and what is about to happen.'

Heikal relayed the message from the British ambassador.

You inquired about the financial arrangements for the Egyptian monitoring committee in Jordan. You asked Heikal to call Sami Sharaf and have him put 30,000 LE at their disposal and indicated that King Faisal and the Emir of Kuwait should also contribute to this sum.

Then you asked, 'Do you remember those verses of poetry that you recited to me during the crisis?'

Heikal repeated the verses, 'I ordered them to where the sun sets / But they didn't see the light till morning / Lost or found, there too go I.'

'Thank God they saw the right course this evening and did not hold on until tomorrow morning,' you said with relief.

Then more quietly, you added, 'For who knows what tomorrow will bring?'

Monday, 28 September

You woke up before eight o'clock and your private doctor came by. After your morning bath you had your shot of insulin and a small breakfast—a single apple from the box that the Lebanese delegation had given you. Then you took your blood pressure, diabetes and heart medications and the painkillers for your legs and had a cup of coffee with your wife. Before you left to the airport for the first official farewell that day, she said, 'The children will all be here for lunch today.'

You asked her about your grandchildren and she said that Gamal (Mona's son) had been there since early morning. His mother had brought him on her way to work so that he could see his grandfather, as you had asked before you went to bed. Hala (Hoda's daughter) was on her way.

You said that you would see them all at lunch and left two minutes before nine for the Cairo airport. You bid farewell to the Lebanese President Suleiman Frangieh at 10.45 a.m., King Hussein at 11.15 a.m., King Faisal at 11.45 a.m., and Nimeiry at 12.15 p.m. and then went home.

At 12.30 you called Mohamed Hassanein Heikal to ask about the most recent developments and said, 'I feel incredibly tired. I don't feel like I can stand upright.'

'Did you see the doctor?' Heikal asked.

'Dr al-Sawy was here. He ran another cardiogram and everything was the same,' you replied.

'And the leg pain?'

You laughed. 'I'll soak my feet in warm salt water and rest afterwards.'

'It was a tremendous effort and I'm sure the president is still in need of a break,' Heikal said.

'I still have to go soon to bid farewell to the Emir of Kuwait. I'll come back after to sleep. I want to sleep for a long time, for a full day or two,' you told him.

Heikal said, 'Is it really necessary for you to go see him off while you're in this state?'

'I have to carry out my duties until the end. In any case, it's the last farewell,' you said. Then you added, 'I might not call tonight if I've already fallen asleep.'

'Sleep well,' Heikal replied.

'Not quite yet. It's still broad daylight,' you said, laughing.

You rested a while in your room. You tried to nap but couldn't get those images out of your head. Scenes of soldiers wandering in the desert struck by Israeli planes, punctuated by moments from the siege of al-Faluja in 1949. The urine you had to drink when the water ran out. The day you married Tahia five years before that. The wedding portrait taken by the photographer Armand. The wedding party where Sayeda Hassan performed her famous song, 'Come on over here my beautiful dear, rose-flower from the garden.' You first home after getting married, in a building on al-Galaly Street in Abbasiya. You carried your bride in your arms up to the third floor, like in the movies. The day Hoda was born, a year later. You named her after Hoda Shaarawi, the leader of the feminist movement. Then came Mona and Khalid in 1949. Meanwhile, the secret Vanguard Organization meetings and gathering weapons that Tahia would hide away in wardrobes before they'd be smuggled to groups of fighters on the canal. Your black Austin car, which you bought with your savings and Tahia's help. Then the Cairo fire and your youngest's illness—Abdel Hamid had been sick when he was only a few months old. And then the night of the coup, which would nearly have failed if not for the daring of the reckless communist Youssef Seddik. The hectic days that followed when you could barely sleep . . . the exhausting negotiations with the British until they finally departed. The conflicts in the Revolutionary Command Council and the problems with the Salem brothers, Salah and Gamal, who were a nervous wreck—Salah completely lost it when the British sent their ultimatum during the Suez crisis but the next moment was eager to fight on the frontlines. This same madness spurred him to take off his belt and whip the writer Ismail al-Habrouk on his bare back. The man died several days later. The shots fired on you by the Muslim Brotherhood in al-Manshiya Square in Alexandria, and which you miraculously survived. In 1955, Abdel Hakim was born and then came the days of glory: Bandung, where you sat beside the giants Nehru, Zhou Enlai and Tito. And when you stood calling out, 'De Lesseps! De Lesseps!' That was the code word to launch the operation to seize the Suez Canal Company and nationalize it . . . the thunderbolt that shook the world and gave you a place among great leaders and heroes. You collapsed afterwards, when the Tripartite Aggression began and you saw for yourself the tanks and planes that had cost more than a hundred million pounds, now utterly destroyed. That day you cried in earnest, then regained your composure and pressed on for the fight ahead. The day the crowds in Damascus lifted your car on their heads. The day you were out in the Mediterranean, after the Iraqi coup in 1958, amidst events even more dramatic than the action movies you loved. The dream of a single vast Arab state had been in sight. The many attempts to assassinate you, which you narrowly survived . . . Your oldest daughter Hoda's wedding day in 1965. How you'd cried when she left the house with her husband. That wasn't the case with her sister Mona the following year when she married Ashraf Marwan—you weren't as pleased about that union. You didn't care for the handsome man she was smitten with, but she insisted on marrying him and you gave in. At the wedding ceremony she surprised you by asking for diamonds as a gift. You'd reminded her of the situation the country was in, but some of the guests who had been invited gathered money for the necklace amongst themselves. Your instincts about the groom quickly proved right. There were reports that he was fond of gambling, and then you found out he owed several thousand dollars to a gambling house in London and that Souad Al Sabah, the wife of the Emir of Kuwait, Sheikh Abdullah al-Mubarak Al Sabah, had paid off his debts. You were furious and summoned Ashraf and his wife immediately to Cairo and gave them a talking to. You asked Mona to divorce him but she refused. She dug in her heels so you let it be. A point of weakness. But you forbade him from coming into your office.

You turned over in bed trying to find a side that was comfortable. There were rumblings in the Western papers and the Saudi-backed newspapers in Beirut. They all crowed that Abdel Nasser was finished and that Israel was waiting for the call from Cairo asking for the terms of surrender.

It bothered you, when you thought about it: A country that puts its affairs in the hands of one man, no matter how great, no matter how many victories he achieves, will always fail. You got dressed again to go to the airport and called Sami Sharaf asking for news. He insisted that you rest. 'I'll sleep when I get back—then I'll sleep for a long time,' you said.

You left your room and headed towards the stairs. You hesitated for a moment in front of the lift and then pressed the button. It was the first time you'd used it to go down. Before you'd only used it going up—going down, you took the stairs.

You left the house at 2.30 p.m. to the Cairo airport and met the Kuwaiti emir, drenched in sweat. At 3.15 p.m. you felt a terrible pain in your chest as you stood beside the emir's plane, waiting for it to take off, felt the sweat cover your whole body. You turned to the person next to you and asked for your car to come to where you were standing because you suddenly felt very tired and wouldn't be able to walk to the car as usual.

You got into the car quickly and asked Mohamed Ahmed to call Dr al-Sawy to meet you at home. You went inside the house, glancing at your little library which you so cherished. You took the lift to the second floor where the whole family was waiting. Hoda had finished work as your secretary, a position she'd held for about a year now. You stood playing with your grandchildren for a moment and then went to your bedroom, calling for your wife to join you. You asked her if she'd had lunch and she said she was waiting for you. As you changed your clothes you said, 'I don't think I can manage anything right now.'

You put on your white and blue-striped pyjamas and lay down on the bed. You called Sami Sharaf asking for the latest news. The call was interrupted by Gamal, Mona's son, who came in asking as he always did for gum or chocolate. You asked Sami to send you some of both because the tin was empty. Then you resumed your conversation—Sami said he'd begin making arrangements for the train from the Saray al-Qubba Station for ten the next morning. At that moment Sami received a message that the Palestinian resistance forces had been intending to blow up King Hussein's plane when it landed in Amman but that the operation had been aborted at your request. You said, 'Thank God. Sami, you know what I think about an eye for an eye.' You asked him to go home for lunch while you rested for a bit.

When Dr al-Sawy came in, your wife excused herself. She was never in the room with you while the others were there, even the doctor.

You said to her, 'Don't worry. I think it's just low blood sugar.'

'Can I bring you anything?' she asked.

'Juice, any kind will do,' Dr al-Sawy said.

She left to prepare a cup of lemon juice and a cup of orange juice.

Dr al-Sawy went out to call Mohamed Ahmed and asked him to summon Dr Mansour Fayez and Dr Zaki al-Ramli. He came back to the bedroom just as your wife returned with the lemon and orange juice.

'The lemon is fresh, but the orange isn't,' she said.

You chose the orange juice and drank it, and said, 'Thanks.'

You recalled when you were a student, acting the part of Julius Caesar in the Britannia Theatre in Alexandria on 19 January 1935, how his life ended at the hands of those closest to him. Those timeless words: '*Et tu, Brute?*' Was that how it was going to end for you, too?

All the moments of greatness flashed through your mind: 80,000 British soldiers finally leaving Egypt after 70 years of occupation. 'De Lesseps! De Lesseps!' The inauguration of the High Dam—the greatest of its kind in the century according to the United Nations, and proof that you had almost achieved your dream for Egypt to become a land of factories and universities and joyous multitudes. Abdel Hakim Amer's face, his warm smile . . . Fahima Hammad . . . the voices chanting your name. How long had it been? Twenty years of continuous struggle, left and right. Had the time come for you to rest?

The doctor immediately diagnosed a heart attack in your anterior arteries, which was dangerous because the heart attack the previous September had affected the posterior arteries.

Dr Mansour Fayez arrived and then Dr al-Ramli.

Their diagnosis was the same and they continued the first aid that Dr al-Sawy had begun as you watched what was happening around you.

Around five o'clock your pulse became more regular and heartbeat returned to normal. At 4.55 p.m. Dr Mansour Fayez told you that you needed to take a long vacation.

You told him, 'I wanted to visit the front first. Can I go and see our boys before this vacation?'

Dr Mansour Fayez said, 'That will be difficult. You can't do anything else before you rest.'

You reached out to turn on the radio to hear the five o'clock news from Radio Cairo.

While the familiar tune that preceded the news report played, Dr Mansour Fayez stepped out to smoke a cigarette. He went to the office and then into the lobby that led into the sitting room, where your wife was waiting, her face in her hands.

'He's all right, thank God,' Dr Fayez said, smiling.

She asked him anxiously, 'Really?'

'You can go in and see him for yourself,' he said.

'I'm afraid of disturbing him. He's not used to me coming in when there are doctors around. He might think something is wrong.'

Then everything changed.

In the bedroom, you were listening to the news brief and then said, 'I didn't hear the news that I was expecting to hear.'

Dr al-Sawy said, 'Why don't you rest, sir? You turned on the radio and turned it off. No need for extra exertion right now.'

You lay back down and said, 'Yes, Dr al-Sawy, thank God, I'm resting now.'

You closed your eyes and your hand slid off your chest. Your face grew calm.

Dr al-Sawy called out for Dr Mansour Fayez in a panic. The doctors crowded around the bed. In that moment, Heikal arrived and was met by the president's wife, who had one hand pressed against her cheek and the other holding her head. He crossed the office quickly to the bedroom where you were lying, the doctors all around you doing chest compressions in a strange silence. Shaarawi Gomaa, Sami Sharaf and Mohamed Ahmed were there too. The electric shock from the defibrillator was repeated and your body shuddered and then became still again.

Ali Sabri arrived and stood there in shock. Then Hussein al-Shafei appeared and turned in the direction of the qibla to pray. Anwar Sadat came and stood before the bed with his face upturned, mumbling verses from the Qur'an. Colonel General Mohamed Fawzi looked on aghast.

'It's over now,' said one of the doctors.

Fawzi said emphatically, 'No, no, that's not possible. Keep trying.' Dr Mansour Fayez began to cry and then the other doctors did too.

At exactly 6.15 p.m. all hope was lost. At 7.00 p.m. the doctors left your bedside, weeping. You wife realized what was going on and hurried into the bedroom. She held your hand and kissed it, and then your daughter Hoda, her sister Mona, Khalid and Abdel Hakim came in. Abdel Hamid wasn't there because he was still away at the naval academy.

Everyone who had left the bedroom gathered in the adjoining office and Anwar Sadat called a meeting in the drawing room.

29 September

We have lost Abdel Nasser.

The pillar of the Arab world has fallen.

Mourners pour into the streets of Beirut,
Damascus, Amman, Tripoli, the Occupied Territories
and throughout the Arab world.

Women commit suicide, cut off their hair, slap
their cheeks.

Nixon cancels Sixth Fleet exercises and declares
from aboard the USS *Saratoga* aircraft carrier off
the Italian coast: 'The world has lost
an outstanding leader.'
(It was as if he was saying: Our work here is complete.)

Dayan orders forces ready for a US-Israeli
intervention to disperse.

Crowds gather overnight around al-Qubba Palace.

All of Egypt was in the streets. Women wore mourning clothes
and young men turned their jackets inside out in their grief and
anguish. Bare-chested men marched, singing the anthem: *Baladi,
baladi, baladi*—Oh my country, you have my heart and my love.
Millions wandered through the streets waving banners embla-
zoned with your image. The streets to your house were over-
flowing. Buses arrived full of passengers; some climbed onto
the bus roofs. Cars and taxis were bursting with people headed
to Heliopolis. Night-shift workers from factories at the outskirts
of Cairo poured out into the streets. Cries came from the cinemas, and thousands rushed forward in a daze. The crowds continued towards Manshiyat al-Bakri until midnight, when news
spread that you were actually laid to rest in al-Qubba Palace so
they headed in that direction. Patients from the Manshiyat al-
Bakri Hospital left their wards and set out towards your home.
Ambulances picked up dozens who had fainted. At 1 a.m. there

were 250 people being taken to hospitals around Cairo. In Sayeda Zainab a woman had a seizure and died of cardiac arrest. In Abbasiya a boy couldn't find space on the bus so he climbed onto the roof as he was slapping his cheeks, lost his balance and fell underneath. By midnight crowds had gathered from all of the areas near Cairo but the train stations in all nearby cities were still packed. The crowds remained around al-Qubba Palace all night, chanting: 'Goodbye Gamal, beloved by millions.'

*

You had forsaken yourself, forsaken us. Then you left, taking all our hopes and aspirations with you—for now.

Author's Acknowledgements

Thank you to friends for their comments and support at various stages of the writing process and in preparing the book for publication: Leila Aweis, Mohamed Taiema, Dr Nadia Muhammad al-Gindi, Dr Iman Yehia, Ali al-Farsi, Hamza Qannawi and Adel al-Gharbawi.

Translator's Note

As a reader of Sonallah Ibrahim might expect, there are numerous archival and historical sources woven into this novel. It was important to Ibrahim that the news clippings be visibly set apart from other elements of the narrative; the fonts and formatting were part of the thoughtful work of editor Sayoni Ghosh. Where possible, I turned to digital archives (especially of the Egyptian newspaper *al-Ahram*), in consultation with the author, to delve into various ambiguities in these fragments. I have chosen to use glosses in some cases, rather than imposing footnotes. Arabic transliterations follow common usages for names, organizations and places, and where relevant and possible, the original English is used for material such as quotes from historical figures or titles of films.